American Indian Literature
and
Critical Studies Series

From the Glittering World

From the Glittering World

A Navajo Story

By Irvin Morris

02287

UNIVERSITY OF OKLAHOMA PRESS : NORMAN

This work combines Navajo traditional stories with fictional names, characters, places, and incidents.

The following chapters were first published, in slightly different versions, as follows: "Squatters" and "August," *Desire and Time: New Work from the Institute of American Indian Arts* (Santa Fe: IAIA, 1990); "The Blood Stone," *Northeast Indian Quarterly* 8, no. 3 (1991); "The Hyatt, the Maori, and the Yanamamo," *Awke:kon Journal* 8, no. 2 (1992); "The Snake of Light," *Circle of Motion: Arizona Anthology of Contemporary American Indian Literature* (Tempe: Arizona Historical Foundation/ Arizona State University, 1990), with permission of the Arizona Historical Foundation/Arizona State University.

Morris, Irvin, 1958–
    From the glittering world : a Navajo story / by Irvin Morris.
       p.   cm. — (American Indian literature and critical studies series ; 22)
    ISBN 0-8061-2895-X (hardcover, alk. paper)
    ISBN 0-8061-3242-6 (paperback, alk. paper)
    1. Navajo Indians—Fiction.   I. Title.   II. Series.
PS3563.0874345F76   1997
813' .54—dc20   96-31861
                                          CIP

From the Glittering World: A Navajo Story is Volume 22 in the American Indian Literature and Critical Studies Series.

Text design by Debora Hackworth.

2 3 4 5 6 7 8 9 10

Dedication

Díí hane' ishlaa 'ígíí éí shimá, bilháájéé', shik'éé dóó shidine'é, bá dooleel. Háálá éí íyisí bitsáádóó óhool'áá'. For my family, my friends, and my people. *Ahéhee'* to all who shared their stories. *Hózhóogo neidá dooleel.* May we all walk in Beauty.

Hózhóogo' éí íishlaa dooleel
Yá'át'éehgo éí íishlaa dooleel
Áyaa díishjí nizhónígo íshlaa
Áyaa díishjí yá'át'éehgo íshlaa

(Prayer)

Contents

T'áá lá í (One). Into the Glittering World   1
  Hajíínéí (The emergence)   3
  Bilagáanaa bi siláo
    (The white officer)   17
  Hwééldi (Fort Sumner)   19
  Diné bi naat'áanii
    (The People's spokesman)   27
  Ná'ii'na' (Comes back to life)   29
Naaki (Two). Child of the Glittering World   31
  Shikéyah (My homeland)   33
  T'áá shábik'ehgo (Sunwise)   35
  Kééhasht'ínígíí (Where I live)   43
  Ma'ii jool dlooshí (Peripatetic Coyote)   49
  Áltsé bináshniihígíí
    (My earliest memories)   53
  Shichei bighandi
    (At my grandfather's house)   55
  Anaa' (Enemies)   63
  Olta' (School)   67

Ahééháshiidi (In the land of
    everlasting summer)   71
Nahashch'idí di (At Badger)   77
Ahééháshiigo nináásísdzá (I go again
    to the land of everlasting summer)   85
Tséhílí
    (Where it flows into the canyon)   99
Nahaghá (The ceremony)   103
Ootííl (It is being carried)   113
Na'nízhoozhí
    (Where the bridge crosses)   117
Shilíí (My horse)   131
Naanish (Work)   139
Yootóódi ólta'
    (The school at Bead Springs)   147
Tóniteel bíighadi ólta'
    (The school by the ocean)   153
Dook'o'ooslííd
    (The San Francisco Peaks)   165
Táá' (Three). Travels in the Glittering World   167
Ha'a'aah biyaadi ólta'
    (The school to the east)   169
Halgaii hatéél (The Great Plains)   177
The Book of the Dead   179
Terra Incognita   187
Díí' (Four). From the Glittering World   193
The Snake of Light   195
Squatters   211
August   219
The Blood Stone   223
The Hyatt, the Maori,
    and the Yanamamo   235
Meat and the Man   245

T'áá lá'í

(One)

Into the Glittering World

Hajíínéí

(The emergence)

*A*lk'idą́ą́' *jiní*. It happened a long time ago, they say. In the beginning there was only darkness, with sky above and water below. Then by some mysterious and holy means, sky and water came together. When they touched, that's when everything began. That was the First World, which was like an island floating in a sea of mist. It was red in color and it was an ancient place. There were no people living there, only *Nílch'i Dine'é*, who existed in spiritual form. They could travel like the wind. There were also *Hashch'ééh Dine'é*, the Holy People, whose form and beauty we have inherited. There was no sun or moon, and there were no stars. The only source of light was the sky, which comprised four sacred colors and glowed with a different hue and lit the world from a different direction according to the time of day. When the eastern sky glowed

3

white, it was considered dawn, and the *Nílch'i Dine'é* would awaken and began to stir in preparation for the day. When the southern sky glowed blue, it was considered day, and the *Nílch'i Dine'é* went about their daily activities. When the western sky was yellow, it was considered evening, and the *Nílch'i Dine'é* put away their work and amusements. When the northern sky turned black, it was considered night, and the *Nílch'i Dine'é* lay down and went to sleep. At the center of that First World, there was a place called *Tóbilhaask'id* where water welled up out of the ground in a great fountain, which was the source of three rivers flowing toward the east, south, and west. No river flowed toward the north, the direction of death and darkness. There were twelve groups of *Nílch'i Dine'é* dwelling in twelve places in that First World, with four groups living in each of the three directions. No one lived to the north. These *Nílch'i Dine'é* had lived there from the very beginning. They were called ants, dragonflies, beetles, bats, and locusts, but they were spiritual beings, not insects or animals. The waters surrounding their world were inhabited by four powerful guardians, *Tééholtsódii* (the Water Monster) to the east, *Dééhtsoh dootl'izh* (Blue Heron) to the south, *Ch'al* (Frog) to the west, and *Ii'ni'dzil ligai* (White Mountain Thunder) to the north. These spiritual beings had lived peacefully and amicably in that world for a long time; but after a while trouble arose, and it was because of adultery. The First World was a holy place, and the immoral behavior of the *Nílch'i Dine'é* angered the water guardians, who did not like what they saw. They did not like the deceit, jealousy, and turmoil that resulted from the de-bauchery. "Do you not like living here?" the guardians scolded. "Do you not value this place? If you cannot behave properly, then you must leave." Three times they were warned by the guardians, but the *Nílch'i Dine'é* did not listen. When they corrupted themselves a fourth time, *Ii'ni'dzil ligaii*, the guardian being from the north, who hadn't spoken before, said, "Because you do not listen, you must depart at once!" But the *Nílch'i*

Dine'é were lost in their wickedness and did not heed. Seeing this, the guardians were outraged and turned their backs on them; they refused to listen to excuses or pleas for forgiveness. The *Nílch'i Dine'é* had to be punished. One morning they saw something on the horizon. It looked like a ring of snowy mountains surrounding them, an unbroken wall of white higher and wider than they could fly across. When it came closer, they saw what it was. The water guardians had sent a great flood. Frightened, the *Nílch'i Dine'é* soared into the air and flew in circles until they reached the sky, but then they discovered that it was smooth and solid. They tried to break through the rigid surface, but they could not even make a scratch. Just as they were ready to give up in despair, a strange blue head emerged from the sky. "Go to the east," it said. The *Nílch'i Dine'é* went to the east and flew through the narrow opening into a blue world, the Second World. There they looked around and saw that the land was barren and flat. They did not see anyone living nearby. Scouts were sent out to see if there were others like themselves further out, but after two days they returned saying they could find no one. But then, one morning, a small group of blue beings appeared. The *Nílch'i Dine'é* saw that these blue beings were like themselves— with legs, feet, bodies, and wings like theirs—and they realized that they could understand their language. The blue beings, who were Swallows, welcomed the newcomers and addressed them as kinsmen. They promised to be friends and allies forever, but before long one of the *Nílch'i Dine'é* took liberties with the head Swallow's wife. That treachery was quickly discovered, and bad feelings immediately arose. "Traitors!" the Swallows cried. "We took you in as friends and relatives, and this is how you repay us? Could this be why you were asked to leave the lower world?" The Swallows demanded that they leave immediately, and once again the *Nílch'i Dine'é* took flight. Once again they encountered a solid sky and could not find an entrance. Just when they were about to give up, a white head mysteriously appeared. "Go to the south," it said. There the locusts led them into the Third World, which was white, through a crooked opening. Again scouts were sent out, and again they found nothing. But in time they discovered that this world was inhabited by Grasshoppers. The *Nílch'i Dine'é* begged the Grasshoppers to let them stay. As before, the hosts addressed the *Nílch'i Dine'é* as friends and kin and mingled with them. All went well for a while, but then one of the *Nílch'i Dine'é* grew weak and committed adultery with the wife of a Grasshopper. The Grasshoppers were incensed and told the *Nílch'i Dine'é* to leave. This time, when they encountered the impenetrable sky, a red head materialized. "Go to the west," it said. When they entered into the Fourth World through a winding entrance hole in the west, they saw that it was black and white. No one greeted them. The land appeared empty. But they saw four great snow-capped mountains in the distance: one to the east, another to the south, a third to the west, and the fourth to the north. The scouts were dispatched to see if anyone lived on those mountains, but they failed to reach the first three. When they went to the northern mountain, however, they returned with fascinating news. A strange group of beings lived there, dwelling in holes in the ground. These were *Kiis'áanii*, the Pueblo peoples, who were living in pit-houses. The *Nílch'i Dine'é* immediately set out to greet the inhabitants of this new land, who welcomed them and pre-pared a feast of corn, squash, pumpkins, and beans. This time, the *Nílch'i Dine'é* resolved to behave themselves. And true to their word, they conducted themselves well, and their days passed uneventfully. Then one day a voice was heard calling from the east. Three times the voice called, each time coming closer. Upon the fourth call, four mysterious beings appeared. They were Holy People: White Body, who is called *Hashch'ééltí'í* (Talking God); Blue Body, known as *Tóneinilii* (Water Sprinkler); Yellow Body, called *Hasch'éélitsoi* (Calling God); and Black Body, referred to as *Hashch'é lizhin* (Fire God). These Holy People did not speak, but they tried to communicate with motions and gestures. However, the *Nílch'i Dine'é* did not understand them. Thus the Holy People appeared, four times over four days. On the fourth day, when the *Nílch'i Dine'é* still could not understand the signs, Black Body finally spoke: "We want to make more people, but in forms that are more pleasing to us," he said. "You have bodies like us, but you also have the teeth, feet, and claws of insects and four-leggeds. And you smell bad. But first, you must purify yourselves before we return." And so the *Nílch'i Dine'é* washed themselves and dried their limbs with sacred cornmeal, white for men and yellow for women. On the twelfth day the deities returned, bringing with them two buckskins and two ears of corn. Blue Body and Black Body carried two buckskins, one of which they laid on the ground. Yellow Body carried two perfect ears of corn, white and yellow, and laid them on the buckskin. The second buckskin was placed over the corn and the *Nílch'i Dine'é* were told to stand back, and the sacred wind entered between the buckskins. As the wind blew, Mirage People appeared and walked around the buckskins. On the fourth turn, the ears of corn moved. When the buckskin was lifted, a man and woman lay where the ears of corn had been. The white ear had been turned into a man and the yellow ear had been turned into a woman. These were *Áltsé Hastiin* and *Áltsé Asdzáán*, First Man and First Woman. These were the first real people, five-fingered beings, and they were made in the image of the Holy People. The Holy People then instructed these new people to build a shelter. First Man and First Woman entered the shelter and thus became husband and wife. First Man was given a rock crystal—the symbol of clear thought—to burn for fire, and First Woman was given turquoise—which represents the power of speech—to burn. In four days a pair of twins were born to them, and these first children were *Nádleeh*, those who have the spirit of both male and female. Only the first pair were like that. In four days another pair of twins were born, and so on. In all, five pairs of twins were born to them. Four days after the birth of the last pair of twins, the Holy People took First Man and First Woman away to the east, to the sacred mountains where they dwelt. There, First Man and First Woman remained for four days. When they returned, the Holy People then took all their children to the east and kept them for four days too. It is during this time that they all received instructions from the Holy People. They learned how to live a good life and to conduct themselves in a manner befitting their divine origins. But because the Holy People were capable of good and evil, they also learned about the terrible secrets of witchcraft as well. After they returned, First Man and First Woman were occasionally seen wearing masks resembling *Hashch'éhooghan* and *Hashch'ééltí'í*. While thus attired they were holy and they prayed for good things for the people: long life, ample rain, and abundant harvests. Those ceremonies were passed on to bless and protect future generations; the prayers, songs, and rituals have not changed from that time. When it came time to marry, the children of First Man and First Woman joined with the *Kiis'áanii* and the children of the Mirage People and others. In four days, children were born to these couples, and in four days those descendants bore offspring also. Soon the land was populated with the growing progeny of First Man and First Woman. They planted great fields of corn and other crops. They also built an earthen dam, and the *Nádleeh* were appointed to be its guardians; while they watched over the dam they created beautiful and useful things, pottery and basketry, and the people praised these inventions. For eight years they lived in comfort and peace. Their days passed uneventfully. Then one day, they saw a strange thing: they saw the sky reach down, while at the same time the earth rose up to meet it. From the point of their union sprang two beings now known as Coyote and Badger, the children of the sky. Their arrival portended both good and bad things for the people. The people prospered for many years, but one day First Woman and First Man had an argument. First

Man was a great hunter and provided much food, but First Woman made an ungrateful remark that insulted and greatly angered First Man. He left her and went to the other side of the fire and remained there all night. In the morning First Man called together all the men and told them about First Woman's insult. "Let's teach the women a lesson," he said. "We shall gather our tools and belongings and move away. They'll learn they can't get along without us after all." The men agreed and gathered up their tools and all the things they had made. First Man, recalling the industriousness of the *Nádleeh*, invited them to come along, and they brought their grinding stones, baskets, cooking utensils, and other useful implements. The men crossed the river and quickly set up a new camp. They cut brush and built new shelters and hunted. When they were hungry, the *Nádleeh* cooked for them. Across the river, the planted fields they had left behind were ripening. Soon the women harvested corn and other crops and made ready for the winter. Their harvest was abundant and they ate well. They pitied the men, who had to do without fresh corn, squash, and beans. In the evenings, they came down to the river and called to the men and taunted them. "How are you getting along over there? Do you remember the taste of roasted corn?" The men had brought seeds with them, but since it was so late in the season, they had not planted. That winter they ate mostly cakes and mush made from the cornmeal that the *Nádleeh* had brought along. The following spring, however, the men planted fields larger than those planted by the women. And this time, without the men's help in the fields, the women's harvest was not as plentiful as before. That winter they did not taunt the men. By the fourth year, the men could not eat all the food they grew, and most of it was left in the fields. The women, however, began to run short of food and soon were facing starvation. They had also begun to miss the company of men. The more brazen used objects such as cacti and smooth stones to satisfy themselves, and some say the monsters that later plagued the people were the result of that practice. In time, First Man realized that they could not live apart forever. He realized that the people were in danger of dying out if they did not reproduce. One evening he called to First Woman and they talked about this. They decided that unless they became one people again they would disappear. So the women crossed the river on rafts and joined the men again, and there was great rejoicing and feasting. However, it was soon discovered that three women were missing, a woman and her two daughters. The people thought they had drowned, but they had been captured instead by the Water Monster, *Tééholtsódii*. The people called to the Holy People for help, and White Body and Blue Body appeared with two shells. They set these shells on the water and caused them to spin, and the water underneath the spinnning shell opened up to reveal the four-chambered dwelling where the monster lived. Accompanied by Coyote, a man and woman descended to the dwelling and searched the chambers—first the one to the east, which was a room of dark waters; then the one to the south, which was made of blue waters; then the one to the west, which was made of yellow waters—and found nothing. Then they entered the north chamber, which was the one made of waters of all colors, and saw the women in there with *Tééholtsódii*. They also saw the children of Water Monster scampering about. The rescue party reclaimed the women and left, but unbeknownst to them Coyote stole one of the Water Monster's children and tucked it under his robe. When they returned, they were greeted joyously and the people feasted again. The following morning, however, the people noticed something disturbing. They saw many animals running past as if fleeing something. All day this went on, and by the third day the commotion had greatly increased. On the morning of the fourth day, they noticed a white light shining up from the horizon. They sent Locust to investigate and he returned with startling news. The strange light was coming from a wall of water that was converging on them from all sides. The people

10

fled to a nearby hill and thought about what they should do. They cried and proclaimed that this was surely their doom. Then one of the people suggested they plant the seed of a tree so they might climb on it and escape the danger. Squirrel produced two seeds, juniper and piñon, and planted them. The seeds sprouted and grew quickly, but the trees soon began to branch out and flattened into squat shapes. Then Weasel produced two seeds also, pine and spruce, and planted them. The seeds grew into tall trees, but they soon tapered into points and stopped growing. The people wailed in despair. But then someone called out that two people were approaching, an old man and a young man. These men went directly to the summit and did not speak but sat down facing east, the young man first and the old man behind him. The old man then produced seven buckskin bags and spoke: "I have gathered soil from the seven sacred mountains in these bundles and I shall give them to you, but I cannot help you further." The people turned to the young man and he said, "I will help you, but you must not watch what I do." So the people left him and waited at a distance. When the young man finally called them, they saw that he had spread out the contents of the bags of soil and planted in it thirty-two reeds with thirty-two joints. He began to sing, and as he did the reeds began to grow, sending roots deep into the earth. The thirty-two reeds fused into one great reed, which soon towered into the sky. The young man told them to enter a hole that appeared on the east side of the reed. As the floodwaters crashed together outside, the hole closed up and sealed tightly. The reed commenced to grow quickly, lifting the people above the rising water. The Holy People accompanied them. When the reed had reached the sky, Black Body secured the reed against the sky with a plume from his headdress. This sky was solid and there was no opening in its surface, so Locust, who was good at making holes, began to scratch and dig. Eventually he broke through, and the people rejoiced. Turkey was the last to climb out, and his white-tipped tail feathers remain to this day as a reminder of their escape. One by one, the people climbed out of the giant reed into this, the Fifth World, the Glittering World.

The flood immediately receded after Coyote's mischief was discovered and *Tééholtsódii's* baby was returned. Again, the people sent out scouts. Finding the land to their liking, they proceeded to dwell upon it, planting fields and making their homes just as in the lower worlds. There were many people by this time and they nearly filled the land. The Holy People performed a test to determine their future. A magic shell was tossed onto a body of water; if it floated, the people would live forever; if it sank, each person would eventually die. The object floated and the people rejoiced, but then Coyote tossed a second stone into the water. It sank, and the people wailed. Then Coyote said, "If we do not die, we shall soon overrun the world. There will be no room for us all." The people saw the wisdom of his words and reluctantly agreed. One morning not long afterward, they noticed that one of the *Nádleeh* had stopped breathing. This was the first death. With instructions from the Holy People, they prepared the body and placed it in a rocky crevice. At about the same time, there was a dispute with the *Kiis'áanii* over the seed corn that had been brought from the lower world, and the groups separated because of it. First Man and First Woman, with the help of the Holy People, marked the boundaries of this new homeland with four sacred mountains made of the soil brought from the lower worlds. Three other mountains were set inside the boundaries. In an elaborate ceremony, the mountains were named and dressed. *Sisnaajiní* was set to the east; it was fastened to the earth with a bolt of lightning and decorated with white shell, white lightning, white corn, dark clouds, and male rain. A cover of sheet lightning was placed over the mountain to protect and adorn it, and Rock Crystal Boy and Rock Crystal Girl were made to dwell there. *Tsoodzil* was set to the south; it was fastened to the earth with a great stone knife, adorned with turquoise, dark mist, and female rain, and over it all was placed a covering of evening sky. One Turquoise Boy and One Corn Kernel Girl were given a home there. *Dook'o'oosłííd* was set to the west; it was fastened to the earth with a sunbeam, ornamented with abalone shell, black clouds, and yellow corn, and the whole was covered with yellow clouds. White Corn Boy and Yellow Corn Boy were settled there. *Dibé ntsaa* was set to the north; it was fastened to the earth with a rainbow and decorated with jet and dark mist, and it was covered with a sheet of darkness. Pollen Boy and Grasshopper Girl were made to live there. The inner mountains were also named and sanctified. *Dzilná'oodilii* was fastened to the earth with a sunbeam, adorned with dark clouds and male rain, and Soft Goods Boy and Soft Goods Girl were given a home there. *Ch'óol'í'ii* was fastened to the earth with a streamer of rain and decorated with pollen, dark mist, and female rain. Boy Who Produces Jewels and Girl Who Produces Jewels were made to dwell there. *Ak'idahnást'ání* was fastened to the earth with a Mirage Stone, ornamented with black clouds and male rain, and guarded by Mirage Stone Boy and Red Coral Girl. In the Fifth World, as in the lower world, the people lived in accordance with the daily cycles of the four changing colors of the sky. But now more light was needed, so the sun and the moon were created. The old man who had helped them escape from the flood in the lower world was given the honor of bearing the sun across the sky, and the young man who had also helped them escape was given the privilege of carrying the moon at night. In return for their sacrifice and labor, they were given immortality and powerful sacred names. In the Fifth World, the people began filling the land and many places were named. The land was rich and the people prospered upon it, but the land soon grew dangerous. *Naayéé'*, monsters, were roaming the land, and they were hunting and eating the people. In time there were only a few people left. These monsters were the offspring of stones and cacti, the result of some women's conduct during the separation of the sexes: *Deelgééd*, the horned monster; *Tsélkáá'adah hwídziiltaal'ii*, who kicked people off cliffs; *Bináá' yee 'aghánii*, who killed with his eyes; and *Tséninahiléeh*, the flying monster who lived atop *Tsébit'a'ii*. In time there were only four people left in the world. These people took refuge near *Tsélgai*, White Rock. First Man went out to pray every day at dawn. One morning he heard a strange sound like the cries of a baby coming from atop *Ch'óol'í'ii*. For three mornings when he went out to pray he heard the sounds coming from atop the cloud-shrouded peak. On the fourth morning, Talking God appeared and instructed him to ascend the mountain. Atop the highest peak First Man found an infant who was *Asdzáán Nádleehí*, Changing Woman, the most beloved of all the deities. He took her home, and because she was holy, she reached maturity in four days. After a time, Changing Woman left to live on *Dzilná'oodilii*. While she was living there she bathed in a waterfall and basked in the Sun. In four days, she gave birth to twin boys, who were the sons of the waterfall and the Sun. They were *Tóbágishchíní* (Born-for-Water), and *Naayéé'neizghání* (Monster Slayer). They quickly grew to maturity also. With the help of the Spider Woman, *Jóhonaa'éí*, and other helpers, the Twins rid the land of the monsters. *Naayéé'neizghání* went out and slew the monsters, while *Tóbágishchíní* remained home and conducted protection ceremonies to ensure victory. One of the last monsters to perish was *Yéi'iitsoh*, the Giant. He was also a son of the Sun; however, because he was killing people the Sun decided to help the Twins to stop him. *Jóhonaa'éí* gave the Twins weapons made of lightning, and he taught them magic that enabled them to travel high over the land on the arching rainbow, which is the road used by the Holy People. After the defeat of the Giant only four monsters remained, Old Age, Poverty, Hunger, and Cold, but the Twins spared these creatures so the people would not grow complacent as immortals. When the land was safe, the Sun asked Changing

Woman to become his wife. She did not consent at first, but after the Sun made promises that she would not be leaving her people forever, she agreed. He built a beautiful house for her to dwell in, on an island in the western sea. Before she left, she made more people by rubbing skin from under her arms and from under her breasts. These were the four original clans: *Honágháahnii, Bit'ahnii, Hashtl'ishnii,* and *Tódích'íi'nii.* Changing Woman took some of these people to live with her, but they soon grew lonesome and they left her home in the western sea to return to *Dinétah.* The Twins left this world to dwell with the Holy People when their work was finished. They left this world from a place where two great rivers meet. They promised that they would always keep watch over the people; it is said that they can still be seen sometimes, floating in the mist above the spot where the waters converge. The Holy People also returned to their home, but they are always within reach through the songs and prayers they gave us. Lastly, a sacred rainbow was placed around *Diné bikéyah,* our homeland, for protection and as a blessing and a reminder of the sacredness of this land. It is said that so long as *Diné* remain within this boundary, we will have the blessings and protection of the Holy People. So long as we remain within these boundaries we will be living in the manner that the Holy People prescribed for us.

Bilagáanaa bi siláo

(The white officer)

The Indian men . . . are to be killed whenever, wherever you can find them: the women and children will
not be harmed, but you will take them prisoners. . . .
if the Indians send in a flag and desire to treat for peace,
say to the bearer; [they have broken] their treaty of
peace, and murdered innocent people and run off livestock: that we are going to punish them for their
crimes, and that you are to kill them wherever they can
be found. We have no faith in their broken promises
and we intend to kill enough of their men to teach them
a lesson. I trust that this severity in the long run will
be the most humane course that could be pursued
toward these Indians.

General James Carleton's instructions to Kit Carson, 1863

Hwééldi

(Fort Sumner)

There is the faint smell of rain on the wind this morning, drifting from the mountains to the west, but it is not likely that we will see any moisture today. The grasses have dried up and merely rustle in useless breezes that torture us with the scent of rains that do not come. The sun is bright and warm, but I do not care to look up at the sky. By noon, the heat will be unbearable. Heat waves will hover like ghosts above the sandy fields. Some of the soldiers have gathered already under the cottonwoods shading the adobe buildings of the fort. They will pass the day watching us, fanning themselves, cleaning their guns, and playing cards. Today will be as long and hot as yesterday, and the day before that.

Níníbaa' is making tortillas over the coals, and there is a jackrabbit roasting on a spit. We are lucky this morning.

19

Sometimes I come back empty-handed from the morning hunt. *Áhálááneeʼ*. It wasn't too long ago that we didn't know what flour was and some people died because we did not know how to use the white powder they gave us to eat. Many old people and children breathed their last clutching their stomachs in agony. Coffee beans were boiled whole and eaten like frijoles. They gave us slabs of salt pork and many people fell ill from eating the rancid fat.

There is a rumor that we might go home soon. Do we dare hope? We have been here four years—a long time to be away from our homeland. We tell them we don't belong here. That we are not meant to be here. There are no mountains. The land does not know us. Here, we have to struggle to coax even a meager harvest from the fields. Back on our homeland, within the protection of the sacred mountains, we were blessed by the Holy People. Life was difficult at times, but we survived because we knew the land. *Diné bikéyah*. The Holy People watched over us. Here, we are outside the protection of the sacred rainbow. We are exposed to the wind. The days pass in boredom, uncertainty, and sorrow. What will become of us? There has been talk that we may be sent further east to *halgaii hatéél*, the land of flatness and great heat, the homeland of our enemies. If that happens, surely we will disappear. There will no longer be *Diné* in the world.

Why don't they see that we are unhappy, that we are suffering, and that we only want to go home? I have never understood why we were brought here. They said we were guilty of raiding and warfare. They accused all of us. That is not right. We knew that many *Diné* had been taken by *naakaai* and *bilagáanaas* to work as slaves. Perhaps some young men did act recklessly and retaliated against those who took their loved ones; but to punish all of us, that is not right. Too much innocent blood has been spilt. My two little sisters died on the way here, and my four brothers died defending them on the homeland, as warriors should. My heart aches to think of them all, especially my mother, who died last year crying out for the homeland.

They told us we would be safe here, that we could start a new life safe from our enemies. They would protect us, they said. The land is fertile, they said. We would raise tremendous crops. Life would be good. We would prosper. It is because we believed those promises that we came. But where are those things? What kind of words do they speak? Do their Holy People look on their deeds with approval?

I had lived just twelve winters when they started coming. At first we didn't believe the stories. That cannot be, we said. Why would they want us to leave? What had we done? We were innocent. We wished no one harm. The Holy People had given us the land to hold forever. Surely they would leave us alone.

But the stories kept coming: they were hunting people like deer, burning fields and dwellings, slaughtering livestock, ruining springs, and cutting down our precious orchards. Every day we saw people, whole camps and individuals, fleeing with just the clothes on their backs. Some were lucky enough to keep their few remaining animals. We did not suspect that we would soon join them.

We moved north to the other side of *Naalyé silá* in the spring, thinking that we would be safe beyond that great wall. There, we joined our relatives at *tséghi'* and planted corn on the canyon floor. We watched the peach trees blossom. The stories had at last begun to fade in our minds when some people arrived with frightening news. We fed them and nursed their wounds. We listened to the stories these walking skeletons told, and the old fear was rekindled.

Still, we felt invincible in our canyon.

That winter was especially bitter, and after the solstice they began in earnest, pursuing people for days on end. The snow was deep, deeper than it had fallen it years, and all the creeks were frozen. The intense cold claimed the young and old, but we could not build fires for fear of attracting attention. The soldiers swarmed like ants. People debated what they should do. We realized we could not plant in the spring, nor could we move our flocks freely. We lived in fear of the soldiers and our enemies who had allied with them.

It was the *bilagáanaa* leader, *Bi'éé'lichí'ii,* who ordered the death and destruction. This man called Redshirt knew that without food we could not hold out for long. We watched as they took what the Holy People had given us. Finally there was nothing left to do but surrender, cold and hungry, at *Chíhootsooí,* in the spring. At the fort, we fell silent. We could not believe our fate. There were hundreds of families already there, stricken with hunger, fear, and sickness, huddled like cornered animals. There was nothing we could do. They had their guns pointed at us. We thought we would be killed at any time. They told our leaders that we had been rounded up because they claimed we were making trouble for the *naakaai* and *bilagáanaa* families who were moving onto our homeland to the east. We learned to our amazement that we were being removed so they might have the land.

We should have listened to those who tried to warn us. We should have done what the *Kiis'áanii* living along the great river to the east asked us to do many years ago. We should have joined them and driven the intruders from our homeland. Then perhaps the *naakaai* and their shiny armor would have never returned from the south to make the *Kiis'áanii* suffer so much. Perhaps then the *bilagáanaa* might never have come with their guns from the east.

My relatives from *Ch'ínlí* arrived in the late summer, having passed the winter in the mountains. They told a story like ours. They had gone north to take shelter on the slopes of *Naatsis'áán,* where they eluded the soldiers for many days, but they were discovered by a patrol of *Nóóda'í* scouts, those enemies from the snowy mountains to the north. In terror they fled south and returned to *tséghi'*, the canyon stronghold, where they took refuge atop an isolated rock. The women and children were instructed to keep quiet, but somehow they were discovered. They huddled behind the trees and boulders dotting the top of the rock, but the soldiers climbed the other side of the canyon and fired at them. Overcome with fear, some people jumped off the cliffs. That was terrible, the way they threw themselves to their deaths rather than feel the bullets. Many others rushed toward the cliffs too, but they were stopped. The elders talked to them and reminded them that life was precious no matter what the circumstances, that they must stay together and look after one another, and that they would survive with the help of the warriors.

I will never forget the journey that brought us here. The evergreens were just beginning to show their reddish winter tinge when we set out from *Shash bitoo'*, a ragged column of people stretching for twelve miles in the snow. I shall tell my children about the horror, and they shall tell their children. We cannot ever forget what happened. In the future, if we survive, we must remember every detail. We must remember that we were made to walk the whole distance in the shadow of their guns. That we were made to bear their contempt in silence. We did not know if we would live from one day to the next. We did not know if we were marching into oblivion.

Only the weakest were allowed to ride on the few wagons and horses they permitted us to take. Many of the old people and the sick were abandoned or shot when they could not keep up. There was no mercy. A pregnant woman was gutted like a deer and left beside the trail. I saw old people, when they could no longer keep up, say to their children, "Go on, leave me here; there is nothing that can be done, whatever happens to me will happen." And later, the guns would boom. There was nothing they could do. Many others died from the cold, dressed as they were in rags. Some died simply because they did not know how to cook the foods they gave us. Others died, I think, because they did not want to go on. They could not bear the thought of leaving. All the way here, for the duration of the journey, there were tears. We wondered if we would ever see our beloved homeland again.

Áháĺaanee'.

This place, *Hwééldi*, is a prison. It is out in the open, with no real shelter from the winds. The soldiers are lucky. They live in adobe houses and are kept warm and well fed. They have raped many of our women. They only laugh when we protest. Prairie dogs, they call us. Gophers! We live in trenches and holes in the ground. A few lucky families have cowhides to use as coverings for their shelters. Most have only rocks and brush to hide behind. Winter is coming and we will have to burrow deeper into the earth. The only wood remaining are the trees shading the soldiers. All the groves along the river have been cut down and even their roots have been pulled out. All the driftwood from the floodplain has been gathered. We have to walk further and further each day to gather mesquite roots for firewood and to hunt.

The men and boys who are not too weak to work are being made to work on the fort. We are building our own prison! Yesterday, I helped to fill the barrels with river water. Today, I am helping to mix adobe for the bricks. Tomorrow, I will help haul the dirt for bricks from the plains. The officers' quarters are finished. The mess hall is lacking only a roof. The barracks and outbuildings are to be built next. The structures are solid and protect the soldiers from the cold as well as the heat. They are lucky.

There is that red-haired soldier that our women despise. He watches them. He has left a trail of blue-eyed babies. We are

24

powerless to do anything. *Ninibaa'* will not leave the hole we live in. Even the land is against us. The water is brackish. The soil is alkaline. We have cleared wide fields, dug miles of irrigation ditches, and planted diligently each spring, but our crops have failed for three years in a row. Drought, worms, grasshoppers, salt, and hail have destroyed our crops. What is happening? What have we done?

The soldiers fail to protect us from our enemies, *Naalání*, who take what they want as we sit helpless out in the open. At night our few remaining animals and our women and children are in danger. Many have been stolen and traded into slavery. We have complained tirelessly about the continuing thefts of our children by the *naakaai* who take them south to dig in the *naakaai* silver mines, but our pleas fall on deaf ears. But until we have fallen completely silent, until it is really finished and the last of us has returned to the earth, we will continue to plead with the Holy People. That is all we can do.

There was a ceremony performed yesterday, *Ma'ii bizéé' nást'á*. Several of the most powerful *hataalii* gathered for the ritual. I did not see the ceremony. I did not even know there was such a thing. It must have been a sight. The people gathered in a large circle, they say. Then the *hataalii* prayed and sang until a coyote appeared and entered the circle. A piece of turquoise was placed under his tongue and he was asked to reveal the truth. In whichever direction he left the circle, that was where our fate would take us. It is said that he ran toward the west, in the direction of our homeland.

Today, at noon, it is rumored there is to be another meeting between our headmen and the *bilagáanaa* leaders. Manuelito, Barboncito, Ganado Mucho, and other *nat'áanii* will speak for us. They have never given up hope. They tell us to be strong. We are all praying that the Holy People will soften the hearts of the *bilagáanaas* and that their decision will be favorable to us, that we shall not be sent east to die on the plains. We shall see whether or not Coyote's message is to come true. We shall see whether or not the Holy People will hear us out here, outside the sacred circle of the guardian rainbow.

Diné bi naat'áanii

(The People's spokesman)

I hope, in the name of the Holy People, that you will not ask us to go to any other country but our own. When *Diné* were first created, four mountains and four rivers were pointed out to us, inside of which we should live, and that was to be *Dinétah*. Changing Woman gave us this land. Our Holy People created it specifically for us.

Dághaa'í *(Barboncito)*
Fort Sumner, New Mexico Territory
June 1868

Ná'ii'na'

(Comes back to life)

Late that afternoon, as the summer sky filled
with rainclouds, the people finally emerged from Tijeras
Canyon, the narrow pass in the Sandia Mountains, and beheld
the wide valley of the Rio Grande below. The river, fringed with
cottonwoods, glittered at the center. That body of water was
their last major obstacle. Once past it, they would reach *Diné
bikéyah* in four days.

In the distance to the west rose a dark mountain swathed
in mist, its high peak hidden in the clouds. A murmur ran back
through the column of people. They gazed at the mountain.
"Could that be our mountain?" they asked each other. "Could
that be *Tsoodzil?*"

An old man at the rear of the column wiped away tears.
A young woman touched his elbow. "*Shicheii*," she said, "is

29

that our mountain?" "*Aoo'*," he answered, nodding. The reaction was immediate and joyous.

"*Áhál´aanee'!*" the people cried. "We are nearly home!"

Naaki

(Two)

Child of the Glittering World

Shikéyah

(My homeland)

From my house, on a clear morning—because we are situated high up on the alluvial apron fronting the Chuska Mountains—I can see a wide sweep of my beloved homeland. From there, I am reminded of who I am: I am not alone, nor am I the first. The land has birthed and sustained all my grandmothers and grandfathers.

Áhálaanee'.

But I have also lived outside the holy rainbow circle and learned of those who do not regard her as a living, sacred entity. Their roots do not penetrate the soil. Perched inside a shiny jet skimming high above the clouds, I have seen my mother, the earth—*Nahasdzáán shimá*—lying below, "conquered."

Outside the circle of the sacred mountains, I have known spiritual hunger and longing for the sound of desert thunder,

33

for turquoise sky, dry air, and radiant sun. And for many years, until I realized what I was doing, I was using hurtful words to describe my mother: *landscape, wilderness, nature.*

The land is ripe with the stories of my people. I can hear their voices on still nights, on summer nights when lightning flashes soundlessly in the distance; on winter nights when the land rests quietly under pristine snow; and in the spring and fall when the mountains speak with a low, murmuring wind voice. I can see their campfires away in the distance, tiny points of light quivering on the plain.

T'áá shábik'ehgo

(Sunwise)

Ha'a'aah. To the east, beyond the broad, nameless valley and the badlands rising on the other side, past the pale sandstone turrets of White Rock thirty miles distant, and the yellow rim of Chaco Canyon twenty miles further, are etched the faint outlines of the Sierra Nacimiento and the Jémez Range, nearly half the state away. Those mountains are sacred to some of my ancestors from Jémez and Santa Clara pueblos who were to live with *Diné* in the years before the Pueblo Rebellion of 1680, and during the Spanish "reconquest" of New Mexico twelve years later, young women who formed new clans within *Diné* society.

From the badlands, the land rises in a gentle incline toward the south in broad, grassy terraces. There, the dark low platform of the Lobo Mesa, a piñon- and juniper-clad formation

35

that occupies most of the southeastern horizon, lifts abruptly from the flat grassland. The cliffs edging the mesa rise from a point directly behind Crownpoint, a BIA agency town located forty miles southeast of my house. Beyond the mesa—over one hundred miles away—rises the bare peak of *Tsoodzil*, our sacred mountain of the south. At its base are the remains of *Yéi'iitsoh bidil*, the petrified tide of blood left where the monster son of *Jóhonaa'éí* was killed by the Twins. The Twins, also sons of the Sun, vaulted into the sky from there on rainbows and sunbeams.

Next on the horizon is *Ak'idahnást'áni*, a square piñon-covered butte that thrusts up out of the plateau summit. This prominence is known as Mirage Stone Mountain in the *Diné* creation story. Mapmakers have labeled it Hosta Butte. From isolated perches atop this towering landmark, sentinels have kept watch on the land since time immemorial. From there, the whole circle of the earth can be seen: *Naalyé silá*, the Chuska Mountains to the west; the San Juan Basin to the north; the rugged snowy ranges of southern Colorado to the northest; and the Rio Puerco Valley and the Zuni Mountains to the south.

Shádi'ááh. To the south, the rounded blue swells of the Zuni Mountains float in perpetual haze. At their northern tip, wedged between the red sandstone hogbacks and the mesa foothills to the north, is the narrow Rio Puerco Valley. In its trough lies the notorious border town of Gallup, New Mexico, a seven-mile-long stretch of bars and nightclubs, tourist traps, gas stations, fast-food joints, Indian jewelry stores, bars, cafés, laundromats, strip malls, and motels.

East of Gallup is *Shash bitoo'*, Bear Springs, now known as Fort Wingate, the point of departure for thousands of *Diné* forced on the infamous Long Walk in 1863. The fort, now closed, was for many years a major ordinance depot, and the large military reservation surrounding it is dotted with thousands of concrete bunkers once used to store ammunition. The land is rocky and covered with piñon and ponderosa pine forests. The numerous canyons eroded into the mountainsides are banded with maroon, white, buff, and gray clays. Ancient *Anaa'sází* settlements, oil refineries, abandoned uranium mines, natural gas wells, recreation areas, and *bilagáanaa* homesteads share the land with hundreds of *Diné* families. At night, orange gas flares lapping the air over refineries light up the valley and the mountainsides.

E'e'aah. To the west, and stretching for fifty miles to the north, are the rugged foothills and the great forested wall of *Naalyé silá*—a name that might be translated as something like "Lying-Down-Wealth." The meaning does not parallel anything in the materialistic Western view, since it refers to the spiritual significance of the range as well as its role as larder and pharmacopoeia. The Chuska Mountains, as they are identified on maps, are the major geological formation on the reservation. They rise to an elevation of nearly ten thousand feet above sea level.

The mountains form an archipelago of well-watered islands in the desert, a stopping-over place for migrating birds. The flat summit supports forests of pine, spruce, fir, gambel oak, and groves of quaking aspen. Numerous ponds and lakes dot the hollows. There are black bear, mountain lion, bobcat, and mule deer. The summit provides the best grazing land on the reservation and we are lucky to have a place there. I spent my childhood summers exploring the woods, learning the names of mountain plants and animals, riding my horse, coming to know the land like a relative. I remember splashing in the ponds; scaling the sandstone cliffs that lift the summit a thousand feet above the lower slopes; picking wild strawberries;

climbing the towering pines; and seeing the brilliant stars crowding the skies at night. I remember listening to the stories told over the snap of campfires—frightening accounts of the feats of *Diné* warriors who battled *naakaai*, the Spanish, and later, *bilagáanaas*. There were also stories about *Nóóda'í* and *Naaláni*, the Utes and Comanches.

Parts of the mountain have various names and stories associated with them. *Bééshlichíi'ii bigiizh*, which is the *Diné* name referring to the reddish chert found there—now known as Narbona Pass—is the major east-west passage through the mountains. The new name is the fruit of many years of work by *Diné* students who petitioned to have the offensive name changed. As far as I know it is the only instance in U.S. history, thus far, where Indian people have been able to influence the change of a placename from something that was seen as offensive to something positive. Formerly, the gap had been known as Washington Pass, named after Colonel John T. Washington, an officer in the U.S. Army who played a major role in an infamous incident that took place in the pass.

In the summer of 1849, Colonel Washington and his troops had been dispatched to *Bééshlichíi'ii bigiizh* to negotiate peace with the *Diné* headman Narbona. Proceedings were going well until one of Washington's officers claimed that he recognized a stolen horse in the *Diné* remuda. The accusation was quickly and vehemently denied. Tensions flared and the negotiation was abruptly halted. Narbona urged caution, but when several *Diné* began riding away, Colonel Washington ordered his troops to open fire. In the ensuing melee, Narbona, sixty-eight years old at the time and a well-known pacifist, was shot in the back.

Naalyé silá is the male partner to *Dzil yíjiin*, Black Mesa, a lower range to the west, which is identified as female. It is said that they lie facing each other, head to feet. Their bodies form a powerful and sacred circle. This relationship reflects the *Diné* worldview in which duality and reciprocity is elemental.

Black Mesa is now being strip-mined. Millions of tons of high-grade bituminous coal are extracted annually to fuel power plants that light up parts of Las Vegas, Phoenix, and Los Angeles. Megawatt power lines carry the electricity right past impoverished *Diné* homes. The companies have renewable leases from the federal government and the mining has continued nonstop since the mid-sixties. The coal is crushed into a powder, mixed with groundwater, and sluiced through huge pipes to the Mohave Generation Station on the Nevada-California border. This slurry-pipeline technology is cost effective for the companies that run the mines, but the operation siphons off millions of gallons of precious water daily from the ancient aquifers under Black Mesa. Natural recharge is modest in this arid terrain, and the toll on the land is immeasurable: the water table at Black Mesa has dropped tremendously. Sacred springs have dried up.

Náhookos. To the north is a sea of grass sloping down from the mountain foothills to the San Juan River, the northern boundary of our homeland. The river itself is hidden below the level of the plains, in a narrow valley choked with cottonwood, tamarisk, Russian olive, and Siberian elm. It is the best agricultural land on the reservation, known for abundant harvests of sweet melons and white and yellow corn. Midway between the river and the mountains rises *Tsébit'a'ii*, the Winged Rock. To the outside world, this basaltic monolith soaring seventeen hundred feet above the surrounding plain is known as Shiprock. It has been featured on innumerable postcards, calendars, and magazines, its twin craggy peaks silhouetted against a red-and-purple sunset. Before it was finally closed to climbers, many *bilagáanaas* lost their lives on its treacherous heights because of unpredictable winds, crumbling rock, rattlesnakes, and fatigue.

It is said that long ago, in some primordial time, the people were in danger and fled to the rock for safety. Like an enormous bird, it rose up and flew away with them. It settled here, its gigantic wings spread to the north and south. Some say it will come to life again, should the need arise.

In the distance to the north are snow-capped peaks. The Henry Mountains in Utah are an encampment of white tipis. Sleeping Ute Mountain near Cortez, Colorado, resembles a large breast, as its *Diné* name, *Dzil abe'*, describes. Mount Hesperus, in the La Plata Mountains of southeastern Colorado, is a mass of frosted stone pinnacles. It is called *Dibé ntsaa*, Big Sheep Mountain, and it is our sacred mountain of the north. Extending southward from behind *Dibé ntsaa* is a distant ribbon of snowbound peaks that culminate in the Mount Blanca massif, *Sisnaajiní*, in south-central Colorado. That mountain is our sacred mountain of the east.

Much closer, below the great ranges arrayed on the horizon, is *Dinétah*, our Holy Land. That is where we emerged into this place, the Fifth World, the Glittering World, as it is known. The actual spot where some *Diné* say the Twins left this world is presently submerged under the Navajo Reservoir, a huge lake formed behind Navajo Dam, an Army Corps of Engineers project that supplies water to the San Juan River Valley, the 110,000-acre Navajo Indian Irrigation Project, and the city of Albuquerque. Southeast of the river is the low, square nub of *Dzilná'oodilii*, Huerfano Mesa, where the Twins—the sons of Changing Woman—were conceived and grew to manhood. *Ch'oolí'ii*, Spruce Knob, the birthplace of Changing Woman, is a few miles away behind the mesa. Across the valley directly east of my home, the Chaco River emerges from between the clay bluffs of the badlands and turns north to join the San Juan River. Forty miles upstream are the silent stone towns of Chaco Canyon: Pueblo Bonito. Pueblo Alto. Pueblo del Arroyo. Casa Rinconada. Peñasco Blanco. Chetro Ketl. Hungo Pavi. Wijiji.

I have seen these landmarks every morning of my life, whether or not I am actually home. These mountains and formations are as real and as alive for me as are the stories that animate them. Better than anything else, they tell me who I am.

Kééhasht'ínígíí

(Where I live)

In summer, the sun rises directly to the east of my home, straight up from between the tan bluffs guarding the mouth of the Chaco River. The bluffs are topped with red clinker, the remains of an ancient fire that swept through coal seams exposed here and there in the eroded hills of the badlands. Depending on the position of the sun, the bluffs are blue-gray, tan, yellow-white, or reddish orange over the course of a day. Groves of salt cedar embroider the riverbanks, and dark green deltas mark the mouths of arroyos feeding runoff from the mountains into the river. In spring and fall, strange birds—storks, cranes, herons, and pelicans—visit the ephemeral wetlands and scattered stock ponds. Their plumage is carefully gathered and used in ceremonies. The badlands are sculpted layers of shales and clays containing fossils, which

43

some say are the bones, teeth and claws of *Naayéé'*. Feral horses and donkeys share that eccentric land with branded Herefords, Brangus, Charolais, Brahma mixes, and Beefmasters. Bobcats, foxes, coyotes, and other predators inhabit those bluffs too, as do raptors such as hawks and owls. In summer, the valley fills with heat waves and the land appears submerged. A brief rainy season, normally in July and August, brings moisture north from the Gulf of Mexico. Now and then a great storm will half-drown the basin and leave it shining with water.

Higher up, on the west side of the valley closer to the foothills where I live, short grasses and shrubs predominate. There is chamisa, four-wing saltbush, pygmy juniper, sacaton grass, Russian thistle, and snakeweed, to name a few. Siberian elm, Lombardy poplar, globe willow, Russian olive, and maples shade newer homesteads. There are hundreds of acres of neglected fields—the legacy of the CCC programs of the 1930s—surrounded by rusted barbwire fences, clogged with sand dunes, reclaimed by greasewood and saltbush, littered with the weather-beaten remnants of windbreaks and orchards.

The village called Naschitti—*Nahashch'idí* in our language—sits beside U.S. Highway 666, a half-mile east of my home and a mile east of the Chuska foothills. Local church groups are agitating to have the number assigned to the highway changed. They blame the cipher 666 for the numerous accidents on the highway—never mind that the reservation is dry and that the highway links two border towns where alcohol is sold. In the village there is a public elementary school and teacherage, a Christian Reformed Church mission, a Catholic church and bingo hall, a trading post, a telephone switching station, water tower, tribal meeting hall, senior citizen's center, tribal police substation, laundromat, greenhouse, low-rent apartments, and a cluster of ranch-style HUD houses. A few private homes circumscribe the village proper.

It is said that a long time ago, there was a drought and the people were suffering. Then one day, a family of badgers digging their burrows in Black Rock Wash struck water and the people were saved. That's how this place came to be known as Nahasch'idí, after the fierce little animal.

The school is dying, the HUD houses are deteriorating, and the scattered trees, shrubs, hedges, and rose bushes have assumed curious postures in their fight to survive. The elevation is six thousand feet above sea level where I live, and the word *steppes* is often used to describe the climate. Summers are hot and winters are cold; temperature swings of twenty degrees or more in an afternoon are not unknown. The average yearly precipitation is about twelve inches.

A dirt road, graded now and then by the BIA Roads Department, veers west from the village. It is infamously rocky. The graders have long since scraped away the thin topsoil and exposed the underlying alluvial rocks and gravel. The white house on your right is my brother's. You can tell he is a miner because the house is new, large, and attractively stuccoed. There is a satellite dish, horse trailers, campers, and a fancy metal corral holding a quarter horse gelding and a buckskin mare. A few yards further sits my cousin's green house with yellow trim. That place has started to go to pieces since he died of a heart attack several years ago. After spending most of his adult life working on sugar beet farms in Idaho, he retired and returned to the homeland—only to last three summers.

My uncle's gray double-wide mobile home is next on the road, along with his neglected cornfield and immaculately kept NAC meeting ground. A *chaha'ooh* sits in the front yard, offering cool shade in the summer and a convenient rack for storing things in winter. After that is my mute aunt's one-room hut. The bus route turns north, and a short road splits off toward the west and the huddle of structures harboring my extended kin.

My mother's house stands out because it looks like a gingerbread house, mocha brown with white trim. A do-good organization painted it those colors over the summer; *bilagáanaa* kids from the east who spent two weeks on the reservation fixing up Indian homes. They wandered about our hovels wide-eyed, bewildered, agog at the condition of our homes. But if anything, they learned that true poverty is unknown to us. There is the land; and we have *K'é*, the intricate and enduring clanship ties that provide us with relatives wherever we go on the reservation; and we have our language, our stories, and our songs.

The older, back part of my mother's house is made of logs covered with chickenwire and stucco, while the front section is made of conventional lumber. This summer we tore out the wallboards in the back rooms for remodeling and found an inscription on the cement chinking between the logs: PETER A. BEGAY, ALL AROUND COWBOY, 1963. The letters, etched into wet cement with a nail, encircled a line drawing of a bull's head. The imprint was so clear it could have been scratched in just moments ago.

The logs of the house have an interesting history. Some of them belonged to my maternal grandmother, whom I never saw. She died in childbirth when my mother was twelve. My grandmother's *hooghan nímazí* was dismantled while my mother was away at Saint Catherine's Indian School in Santa Fe. When she returned years later after my grandmother's death, she was able to locate only a few of the logs. The rest had simply disappeared. The other logs in our house were hauled from the mountains by my mother and her first and only husband after their wedding. They chopped down ponderosa pines and smoothed and shaped the timbers by hand. She took the logs with her after their divorce and had the house reassembled at my grandfather's place, where we lived for a while. But tensions between her and my grandfather's new wife forced her to once again dismantle the cabin and move us to the foot of the mountains where we now live. It's been our home for over thirty years. Four generations have lived in it: my mother, my siblings, my nieces and nephews, and now their children.

Tóbaahí nishłí, doo Tótsohnii éí báshíshchíín. That is the proper way to introduce and identify myself. I am of the Edgewater clan, and I am born for the Big Water clan. I belong to my mother's clan because we trace our lineage through the female line. Anyone who is *Tóbaahí* is thus part of my family. We don't go strictly by biological descent. That is, my family doesn't just include my nuclear family but comprises everyone who is *Tóbaahí*. Not only that, but everyone who is *Tótsohnii*, my father's clan, is related to me also. What this means is that through the clan system my "family" is very large, and chances are that wherever I go on the homeland I will meet someone who is my relative. If I were to be stranded away from home, for example, I could count on my clansmen to help. In turn, I have that obligation too. The most important thing is that we are never alone. We are parts of large groups, which are in turn strands in the web making up *Diné* society. Knowing your clan weaves you inextricably into that web. Knowing your clan also ties you directly into the *Diné* creation story, because all the clans are descended from the four original clans that were created by Changing Woman from her body.

My mother is born for *Hanághááhnii*. Our neighbors are also *Hanághááhnii*, related to us through her father's clan. That circumstance is unusual but not unknown. Normally a woman lives near her mother and her sisters, as *Diné* are matrilineal and matrilocal. When my mother's mother died in childbirth, her maternal relatives were obligated by blood and kinship ties to look after her and the six other children. But none of them were in a position at that time to take in extra mouths, so they went to live with their paternal aunt at a locality called *Nahashch'id hayáázh*, Little Badger. That is where I spent most of my childhood. That tiny old lady was descended from a Zuni captive, and her name was *Bilgííbaa'*, One-Who-Fought-the-Enemy. *Diné* women are given names referring to war. Their stirring sticks, given to them by the Holy People and used to make cornmeal mush, are powerful symbols and weapons against hunger.

Ma'ii jool dlooshi

(Peripatetic Coyote)

One day, Coyote was trotting along when he happened upon Doe and her frisky fawns. Right away, he noticed the beautiful speckled coats that the fawns wore. My, he exclaimed, how lovely! But Coyote, being the shallow person that he was, quickly grew envious. He wanted apparel just as pretty, if not prettier, for his own children. Their motley coats were certainly dull by comparison. He sighed, wishing they had inherited the magnificent hues of his original coat, which he had lost when a wicked trick backfired. He had wandered around naked until some chipmunks took pity on him and gave him an old discarded coat they had found. His children had inherited that lackluster garb. As usual, Coyote hadn't learned from that experience. A scheme was taking shape in his mind.

"*Dooládóó' niyázhí danizhóní da*," he said, glancing at the fawns.

"Thank you," answered Doe. She acknowledged his compliment graciously, but she knew his reputation and was wary.

"I wish my own children had pretty coats like that," he said. "Though I love them dearly, I am the first to admit that they are rather drab."

Doe had noticed his covetous glances at her fawns. She was no fool. She saw the greedy look in his eyes and she knew that something was on his mind. She smiled at him demurely.

"Tell me," said Coyote, growing bold. "How did you get such gorgeous attire?"

"Well . . ." she said.

Coyote's ears rose. "Yes?" he said, a bit too quickly. Sometimes he was too eager for his own good. "Please, do tell."

"It wasn't easy, but if you really want to know—"

"Yes?" Coyote said, barely containing his excitement.

"Of course, you have to understand how special those coats are," Doe said, gazing fondly at her fawns frisking nearby, "and how difficult they are to come by. They're not for just anybody . . ."

Coyote's eyes gleamed; he was already imagining the compliments he'd get: "*Nizhóní!*" "How lovely they are!"

Doe saw the rapturous look on his face. She knew he was beyond help then.

"As I was saying," she said, flicking her ears to get his attention, "they're not easy to come by. You have to be really sure you want them, and you must be willing to endure some hardship. You must be willing to pay the price."

Coyote didn't hesitate a bit. "Anything," he said. "Anything at all."

"Okay, then. I obtained those beautiful coats like this: First, I built a roaring fire in my outdoor oven. Then when the stones of the oven wall started to glow red, I placed my fawns inside and sealed the opening shut with mud. They stayed in there overnight, and by morning they had turned a beautiful brown color, with white spots scattered like stars on their backs."

"Thank you," said Coyote, trotting off. "Thank you very much." Coyote went straight home. He wanted those coats very badly. He built a roaring fire in his outdoor oven. He fed wood to the fire until the stones glowed. Then Coyote gathered up his children and placed them inside the oven. He ignored their cries and sealed the oven shut. In the morning, he broke open the seal and looked inside expecting to see his children in beautiful new coats. Instead, he saw that they had all been burned to a crisp.

Áltsé bínáshniihígíí

(My earliest memories)

The bird's nest is tucked into the eaves of the house. The eaves are painted white and the house is made of buff-colored sandstone. It is summer and the sun is very hot. Across the river, the red-topped bluffs shimmer in the heat. They look as if they are on fire. It is quiet under the *chaha'ooh*. The sand is cool to the touch. The blocks of wood that are my cars are motionless for the moment.

Inside the house there are low, female voices. Now and then someone moves past the window.

The bird's nest is made of grass, horsehair, bits of wool, and twigs. Excited chirpings greet the parent birds when they return. They bob into the nest, shake their tails, look around, and fly off again.

53

It is night. My mother and older brother have left me alone. They have gone to check on the sheep. It is lambing time, and the corral is on a hillside a quarter-mile away. They must make sure the newborn lambs, if any, have not been rejected and are feeding properly. If a ewe has neglected her lamb, it must be brought inside.

I am little and my mother has told me to stay put. It is cold outside and I can't walk fast enough to keep up. I listen to Patsy Cline on the radio and watch the curtained window and the wooden door. Flames crackle loudly inside the stove made from an old metal barrel with one side cut out. A kerosene lamp adds more light.

After a while, I decide to follow.

I make my way along the trail in my bare feet. The night is pitch black and I make my way more by feel than by sight. In a while I reach the corral and see the two flashlights bobbing among the milling sheep. I climb over the side of the corral and approach my mother. She is surprised. "What are you doing here?" she says. She is surprised that I have followed them all that way in the darkness. "Don't you know what you might run into out here?"

I am three years old.

Shichei bighandi

(At my grandfather's house)

It is winter. We are living south of my grandfather's house, about two miles west of the stone house. The
drought is over finally and we have moved back from the river
and the lowlands. We live in a one-room cabin. There is only
my mother, my sister, and I. My brothers are away at Stewart
Indian School in Nevada. It is a peaceful time. One night, I
get a bug in my ear. I hear it scrabbling around inside. My
mother borrows a flashlight from my grandfather to check.
Choosh léi' át'ééla, she says. She uses a hairpin to pull out a
black, spiderlike thing. I remember it looking like an octopus,
though I didn't know that word then.

That summer, my sister and I almost killed our cat. We had
placed a rubber band around its neck in play and forgotten it.

The rubber had eaten into tender flesh by the time my mother discovered it. That was Sylvester, a black-and-white *mosí*. I remember the gummy flesh and the sharp smell. The hair never grew back on his neck, and as long as he lived he wore a collar of pink skin.

Once in a while we went to see movies at the Chapter House, which is the seat of local government, and sometimes if it was a scary movie, I'd have nightmares. The popcorn and candy the teachers sold lured us too, but there was a big tradeoff. Even the Three Stooges' pranks with a plastic skeleton had me hiding on the floor with my eyes tightly closed and my hands clapped securely over my ears.

One night we are in a *hooghan* for a ceremony. A man wants to know why he is ill and we are gathered there to find out. The *hataalii* prays and sings. When he stops, the lamps are extinguished. We sit in absolute darkness. In the far distance, we hear other voices praying and singing too. Don't say anything, warns the *hataalii*. Listen very closely. See if you can identify the voices. They are the ones causing your sickness. The voices fade and we strain to hear them.

Suddenly there is a noise outside, a thump, and a sudden rush of wind. They know we are doing this, says the *hataalii*, but don't be afraid, pay them no mind. Then there are gasps. An image slowly materializes in the blackness at the center of the room. It is the dim figure of a man, floating in the air. I do not know him, but there are murmurs of recognition from the others in the room.

Years later, I am visiting a relative who accidentally drops some photo negatives and I pick them up. The memory of the image hovering in the darkness inside the *hooghan* flashes back when I see the ghostly reverse images on the film.

A daily terror at that time was a mean wether with one curled horn. It was so spiteful because my older brothers had teased it so much, pricking it with a stick, pulling its tail, but it didn't bother to charge them because they were fast and could easily dodge its attempts or outrun it. Whenever it saw us, however, my sister and I, it tucked its ears back and stamped its feet. We were easy prey, small and timid. It once butted my mother when she was bent over a ewe, helping a lamb to nurse. She whirled around, picked up an enamelware pan that was used as a dog dish, and slammed it over the wether's head. The wether, dazed and shaking its head, backed away and vanished into the flock. It left us alone after that, but we knew it watched us all the time with its yellow slitted eyes. Months later, my grandfather donated the wether to a ceremonial feast and it was carried away, its feet bound with baling wire, in the back of a truck.

My grandfather's favorite dish was *atsiits'iin*. Roasted sheep's head. He would build a fire to singe the wool from the bloody head, tuck the lolling tongue back into the mouth, scoop aside the embers, and bury the head in the heated earth. In a couple hours the feast would be ready. He'd pull out the steaming head, scrape off the dirt, place it on the table, and pour coffee. The tongue was a delicacy, as were the eyes, cartilage, and brains. I was always fearful of the grotesque charred head, especially if it had horns. Years later, that's what I pictured when the missionaries talked about the Devil.

Sometimes I accompanied my brothers when they took the sheep to the artesian well about two miles away near the river.

One time, we decided to steal some melons from a field along the way. We snuck down a wash and managed to make it into the melon patch. We thought we had made a successful raid until one of my cousins yelled that someone was coming. We dropped the melons and ran, but the rider caught up with us easily and whipped our legs with her baling-wire crop. She was the daughter of the man in the stone house. Her name was Juanita. She broke horses and never married. Her face was smeared with red ocher and mutton fat, the old-time sunblock.

Every summer we took our sheep to the local sheep dip to rid them of lice and other parasites. It was a community event and for that reason we all looked forward to the day. The people would bring their flocks from miles around. Some of them numbered in the hundreds, and when they moved they raised towering clouds of dust. They came pouring out from between the surrounding hills like frothing rivers of storm water churning and swirling over the brown-and-yellow earth. There was the incessant bleating of lambs and kids, the tinkle of bells, and the barking of sheep dogs. Billy goats and rams made trouble for everyone. People on horseback rode to and fro, keeping the flocks from straying or mixing. Women opened brightly colored umbrellas and gathered for gossip, clustered like blossoms alongside the corrals or beside campfires that filled the air with the delicious smells of boiling coffee and roasting meat. Groups of men gathered in the shade under pines to tell jokes and play cards. An enterprising family would sell pop and ice cream from the back of a truck. Young people affected indifference and tended to food and animals with exaggerated care, all the while sizing each other up. The BIA livestock manager for the local grazing district, a man called *Bijoochii'*—a name referring to his ruddy coloring and similar to the word for a bodily orifice—would dump the medicines into the steaming water. Then the men would throw the panicked sheep and goats into the water, where they would bleat and bawl as they swam from one end of the vat to the other, assisted by women wielding hooked aspen poles. Now and then a lamb or kid would drown and *Bijoochii'* would scoop it out with a hook and throw it aside with a plop. The drenched animals would clamber up the other side, where they would shake themselves and fill the air with flying water.

Every day, my mother would fry potatoes. Red potatoes, white potatoes, brown. We lived on potatoes and flour tortillas because they were cheap and filling. A simple hamburger was a delicacy we enjoyed only on those rare occasions when my aunt's husband, a member of the tribal council, treated us in town. Each morning I would wake to the sound of my mother stirring the ashes in the stove, and then the roar of the fire as it rose up the stovepipe. Above the crackling of the fire I'd hear her humming to herself or singing along with the radio as she peeled potatoes. Then there'd be the spatter of hot grease as she dumped the slices into the pan. For variety, she sometimes added mutton, onions, canned corn, eggs and bacon, or pork and beans to the potatoes. Sometimes she added flour and water to make a gravy. She could make the potatoes soft and mushy or golden and crisp. She might slice them thick or thin, into cubes, or like hashbrowns. Once in a great while she would buy a can of corned beef or Spam to add to the potatoes. My favorite, though, was potatoes fried in a cast-iron skillet over an open fire. That dish has the power to bring back memories.

My grandfather told of a time when *bilagáanaas* drove past on the highway in jalopies piled high with their worldly belongings. They were looking for work in the midst of the Great Depression. They would drive past in their misery and cast glances at our ripening fields. They would sometimes stop to beg or barter for food, trading their meager possessions for corn, squash, and melons. In that way, sewing machines, wedding gowns, coffee grinders, and other artifacts of "civilization" made their way into local homes.

One summer, a truck carrying a load of pigs overturned on the highway and two hundred animals escaped. By fall, many local *Diné* had become pig farmers. Within four years, the pigs were multiplying and the people were tired of pork. The boars began biting people and eating chickens and lambs. That settled the matter. In a while, most of the pigs had been butchered, and only the tusks and the stories remained. My grandfather told of the spotted pigs he had once owned, and of the way they tasted in a big steaming dish of posole.

In the summer, my grandfather and brothers would take their rifles and hunt prairie dogs in the afternoon. This wasn't easy becuase the little rodents were ever alert for danger. A lookout's warning bark would cause a whole colony to disappear for hours. Still, the hunters always seemed to return with a string of fat tawny *dlóó'* dangling from their belts. Grandpa would gut them and stitch the carcasses shut with string, then he'd build a roaring fire to singe the hair off. After the fire died down he'd sweep aside the ashes and dig a pit to cook them. A couple hours later he'd uncover the steaming cache and lay the feast on the table. Their tender and succulent flesh would melt off the bones. Hot coffee, roasted corn, fried squash, fresh chilies, and Grandma's warm tortillas would complete the meal.

My mute aunt would put on her galoshes and go out into the fields after a particularly heavy rain when streams of runoff crisscrossed the land. She'd work for hours, shoveling, making dikes and trenches to divert the water into the burrows. After a half-hour or so, the drowned animals would float up. Her specialty was *dlóó'* baked to juicy perfection: moist on the inside, crisp and golden on the outside.

There's a story about two men from the old days when people from the reservation were just beginning to venture into the outside world. In those days it was a common practice to pack a lunch for long journeys. These men were traveling to Window Rock for tribal business. Noon found them at a bordertown café, where they took their bag lunches inside and ordered black coffee. The *bilagáanaa* waitress was startled to see, when she returned with their cups, that they had unwrapped their lunches and were feasting on roasted *dlóó'*. Horrified, she fled into the kitchen to tell the cooks that those Indians out there were eating puppies!

Anaa'

(Enemies)

Somewhere in the badlands lie the bones of a group of *anaa'*, enemies who had been ambushed and killed sometime in the 1800s. No one knows who they were, or what their destination had been. The story is that they were discovered passing through the area in a time of warfare and were attacked and killed. The outside world has forgotten them, but generations of *hataalii* have kept an eye on the remains over the years. The location of the site is kept secret. There is good reason to keep the curious away, for these bones are dangerous. They hold power that can injure ordinary mortals, and only *hataalii* and the initiated can safely approach them.

In one of our major ceremonies, *Ndáá'*, the Enemyway, a fragment of bone taken from the site is ritualistically killed again. The bone is called a captive and treated as such. It is

63

lashed to a stick. On a certain day, it is taken away from the ceremonial *hooghan* and stunned with ash before one of the men shoots a bullet into it. I have never seen that part of the ceremony. Only the men who will do the actual killing are allowed to go. I have never been to the site nor would I want to, so great is my belief in the danger.

Ndáá' is a summertime ceremony used to purify and reintegrate warriors back into society after they have been away in battle. The ceremony also has other uses. It is used to purify and reintegrate anyone who has been away among outsiders. It is known that physical and spiritual illness results from contact with non-Indians. Hair is used if bones are not available. One of my uncles carried around an envelope containing a snippet of the blond locks of his Parisian girlfriend for many years. In case he got sick from his contact with her, he said. My grandmother was scandalized.

It is winter. The fires are lit at dusk, two parallel rows between which the dancing will take place and around which the people will gather. Great piles of wood that will feed the flames throughout the night loom behind the fires. They will also serve as grandstands for spectators once the dancing begins. Women cluster near them, wrapped in Pendleton shawls and glittering with silver. The men, too, are dressed in their finest. In the darkness beyond the reach of the firelight, young lovers meet and talk. The ceremonial *hooghan* sits at the west end of the dance ground, and to the east, just beyond the reach of the the fires furthest from the ceremonial *hooghan,* another fire flickers inside a circular enclosure of piñon boughs. Mysterious shadows move around that fire. Elders sip hot coffee and reminisce. Young mothers sooth crying babies, and children play and chatter. Inside the ceremonial *hooghan* there is singing and long, complicated prayers. Now and then the burning wood shifts and releases galaxies of glowing sparks into the air.

Sometime past midnight there is a high-pitched cry and the people hush. The *Yéi'ii* have arrived. They emerge from the enclosure and slowly enter the dance ground, their bells tinkling, led by *Haashch'ééltí'í*, Talking God. Eagle feathers surround his mask like the rays of the sun. He wears a buckskin cape, a foxtail, and boughs of evergreens. Behind him are the rest of the pantheon, bodies painted with white clay, carrying gourd rattles, boughs of spruce tied around their necks and wrists, kilts glittering with silver, foxtails bobbing behind them. Beside them are female *Yéi'ii* who wear velveteen and satin, silver and turquoise. In the firelight, the streamers of colorful ribbons attached to their backs and elbows flutter and sweep to the earth like rainbows arching out of clouds. All the *Yéi'ii* wear painted masks. They are otherworldly in the moving light of the campfires, and their falsetto voices rise again and again as they dance. At the rear is *Tóneinilii*, the Water Sprinkler. He runs around making sacred laughter, teasing the *Yéi'ii* as well as the spectators. He subjects those who had committed moral transgressions to shame and ridicule, chides laziness or greed, or simply does outrageous things to invoke the healing power of laughter.

The dancing goes on until dawn, when the *Yéi'ii* finally leave to return to their home, with the understanding that they will come again the following year. The people bless them with sprinkles of pollen as they file past. The bluebird song accompanies their retreat. When they are gone, people draw the holiness of dawn into themselves with sweeping motions of their hands and sprinkle pollen toward the east. Then it is finished, and slowly the fires turn to smoking ash and the people leave the holy ground.

It is my first Halloween. My brothers are in school and come home with that idea. We get dressed up in rags and paper masks and go to a neighbor's house. The old, old lady living there scolds us because she thinks we are taunting her. She swings her cane at our legs even as we try to explain about Halloween.

The wife of the man in the stone house gives us jawbreakers and sticks of gum. Another neighbor gives us gingersnaps. At the school compound, the teachers give us candy bars, popcorn balls, cookies, and apples. We are overwhelmed and go home with paper bags bulging.

Olta'

(School)

Mrs. R taught first grade. She liked to put pomade in my hair and part it on the left. She would recite the alphabet with a tremulous voice, her big pale arms making swooping motions in the air as she wrote invisible letters: "A-is-for-apple, B-is-for-baker . . ." As she did this, the undersides of her arms would ripple like windblown puddle water. I never exactly caught on to what she was doing, but I swung my own arms in imitation. Still, I felt bad because I was cheating; no matter how closely I watched, I could not fathom the shapes of the letters, whereas the other kids churned their arms easily and sang out the letters. "D-is-for dog . . . C-is-for-cat."

She hung pictures, expertly colored ditto sheets of animals, people, and things, above the blackboard. T-is-for-trout was my favorite because of the beautiful job Mrs. R had done coloring the fish. We colored other pictures, B-is-for-boy and G-is-for-girl, with yellow hair and blue eyes. Oddly, it never seemed to have occurred to Mrs. R that we might color the pictures differently—like ourselves, with brown skin, brown eyes, and black hair.

Every morning, we recited the Pledge of Allegiance. Only, sometimes when we said "the United States of America," we said it this way: *"Yoodíyáhéedi dibé yika,"* which means, roughly, "The sheep are grazing near my ex's place." Though we were young, we understood that relations with estranged lovers and in-laws could be thorny. We also liked to say, *"Bilagáanaa bilasáanaa bil likan,"* a tongue twister meaning "White people like apples." The meaning did not have negative connotions back then. We were afraid of Mrs. R, who was the first *bilagáanaa* we had known, and we regarded her with a mixture of awe, fear, and curiosity. She had a smoker's cough, the beginnings of a dowager's hump, and a head of tightly curled and dyed lackluster brown hair. She wore dresses that rode up in back when she bent over to pick up something and showed the backs of her fleshy knees bulging over the tops of her rolled-down hose. She made the best cookies in the world, but she could also punish us, smack her ruler against our palms, put a spoonful of soap in our mouths, or deliver a burning swat on our behinds with the paddle she kept in her desk. We were especially terrified because that kind of discipline was unknown to us at home.

She once put soap in my mouth for telling, in all innocence, about how my mute aunt and her boyfriend made her bed squeak when he visited at night. "Nasty!" she said. "Dirty!" She got even more mad when I threw up from the green liquid soap.

My cousins and I frequently slept over at my aunt's house because she was kind, she had no small children, and she liked having us around. She would chase us as we shrieked and fled in mock terror. Sometimes she would sprinkle cedar incense on the hot top of the woodstove and bless herself with the smoke. We would imitate her as the fragrant *iyahdadi'nil* curled up and enveloped us. She cooked for us and covered us when we fell asleep. Occasionally she would darken her eyebrows with a pencil and put on lipstick. She kept count of the phases of the moon, and we often sat with her outside watching the great yellow moon rise up from the badlands and float into the sky. We slept on her spare bed, huddled like puppies.

The story is that when she was very young she played too near an anthill and was stung hundreds of times. The venom swelled her eyes shut, nearly closed her throat, and bloated her limbs hideously. The trauma caused her to lose the use of her tongue.

Ahééháshiidi

(In the land of everlasting summer)

In Yuma, a Quechan girl with white plastic eyeglass frames looked down her nose at me. He's a *Navajo*, she'd say, her voice dripping with disdain. She never let me use the teeter-totter or the swing. She made faces and threw dirt at me. I avoided her because she was big and fat and kicked like a horse. I hung around with the Mexican kids, the ones whose parents worked in the fields. We called her "Gordita" and made her cry by mimicking the way she pushed her eyeglasses up with one finger.

Calvin G, who was notorious for doing "nasty things," wasn't shy about pulling up her dress, slapping her behind, or grabbing her between the legs. She'd shriek and swing her arms, but she couldn't run fast enough to catch him. He'd jeer at her from a distance and tug at his own crotch. He told us

71

some amazing things about men and women. Grownup men had organs sharp as pencils and women had teeth down there, he said; they got stuck together like dogs and had to be pulled apart. He lived in a four-room apartment with his parents and ten siblings.

Mrs. H found out about those stories and made him tell. She didn't stop there, unfortunately. She made him demonstrate what he meant. "Young man!" she shrieked when Calvin walked up to her and humped his little body against her. He didn't even reach her chest. She sputtered and turned rosy pink. "Take me, Lord!" she said, her hand clutched to her chest, her face tilted up toward heaven. We got sent home. My Christian grandfather whipped me with a wire coat hanger, declaring, "Spare the rod and spoil the child!" The worst punishment I ever got from my other grandfather, the one who was a medicine man on the reservation, was a scolding. Other times it was a stern look, or icy silence.

We lived on Indian Hill, across the street from the PHS Indian Hospital. The town of Yuma was across the Colorado River. My grandfather was the maintenance supervisor and my mother worked as a nurse's aide. The hospital was on the Fort Yuma Indian Reservation in Winterhaven, California. The old Yuma Territorial Prison sat on a hill across the river, above the town and the surrounding orange groves. I went to the prison museum now and then and wandered through the open-air corridors between the empty cells, wondering what it might have been like being locked up there in the hellish summer heat when the metal bars could inflict a serious burn if touched. Tourists often lingered by a small pile of rocks near one corner of the prison grounds. The museum claimed it was the grave of Billy the Kid.

The hospital and support buildings occupied most of the flat area atop Indian Hill, but there were also apartment buildings, government offices, the mission, and a day care center. Our house, which had once been the physician's residence, was immense. There was a huge backyard with date palms and flowering shrubs, red and lavender azaleas. The lawn was fierce with stickers, and the mulberry trees shading the walk to the back gate dropped fruit that stained the concrete purple in summer. The family dog, Tippy, and I found many hours of relief from the heat playing with the lawn sprinklers. Surrounding us on all sides at varying distances, jagged chocolate-colored mountains floated on heat waves above the desert floor.

My best friend, after I was forbidden to see Calvin G, was Ezra O, a Cocopah. We liked to sneak down to the river and explore the maze of trails winding through the tangled brush on the banks, though my mother warned us about the hoboes who camped down there. Once, we surprised a naked *bilagáanaa* man taking a bath in a secluded cove on the river. He rose up out of the water and stood glistening and dripping in the dappled sunlight. We stood stock-still, staring, until he yelled at us and we ran. He was deathly pale, except for his hands and face, which were brown. He was fearsome, with his furry body, bushy black beard, and booming voice.

We would lie on the bridge over the river and count the catfish hanging motionless in the water below. We also went to the mission across the street, which was home to nuns in blue-and-white habits. They never spoke, as far as we knew, and they had a beautiful garden courtyard. They grew enormous fragrant roses there, and sweet oranges and tangerines. The sunny slope behind the mission was covered with groves of prickly pear cactus. The trail to the river wound between them, so you had to be careful going down. The railroad ran just below the hill too, and when we heard the train coming, we'd run to the edge of the hill and count the passing cars. Often, late at night, the train would wake me and I'd lie there listening to its passing.

Raphael's grandmother, who always dressed in black, and whose apartment always seemed to smell of moldy oranges, was the sweetest grandmother I've ever known. Her name was Domatilla and she spoke only Spanish, but I understood her perfectly. She was small and dark and always covered her head with a black scarf. She made flan and biscochitos and other sweets. There was a small altar with candles in their living room. Old, yellowed photographs in ornate silver frames hung on the wall: stern-looking men with black eyes and handlebar mustaches, solemn-looking women posed stiffly in front of painted backdrops of fanciful gardens and landscapes.

One day, my grandfather was going to a co-worker's house. I always tagged along wherever he went. If I had known what he was going for this time, however, I would have run the other way. I hopped aboard our white station wagon like we were going to town. Instead, we drove into the desert. "You'll have to stay in the car," he said. We flew past cholla cactus and mesquite, ocotillo and saguaro. Cramped jacal huts surrounded by rusted cars appeared here and there amid the paloverdes. A half-hour later, we pulled up to a cluster of houses and were greeted by Francisco. He and my grandfather greeted one another and spoke in low voices. When they turned to walk away, my grandfather motioned for me to stay in the car, but I followed as soon as they disappeared from sight.

The people had assembled around this pyre. I didn't know what it was. I thought is was just a pile of wood. Nothing was happening, as far as I could tell, but after a while the wood was set ablaze. The yellow-and-orange flames quickly engulfed the wood and smoke poured off it in thick ropes. People crowded in front of me so I couldn't see clearly. I hung back, partially hidden behind a car, afraid to let my grandfather see me. Somehow he discovered me anyway and pulled roughly on my arm. "I told you to stay in the car," he scolded. As he began to pull me away, there arose a commotion. Frightened, I pressed my face into his side as he led me away. When I looked back a few steps later, a gap opened momentarily in the wall of people and I noticed that the fire had begun to collapse. That's when I saw the body. The skull actually, amid the flames. I will never forget the sight, and the stench that suddenly engulfed us. I had nightmares about that for months afterward until my mother finally had to have a ceremony done for me when we returned to the reservation. I had violated the taboo against contact with the dead.

Nahashch'idi di

(At Badger)

I was twelve and afflicted with the agonies of full-blown puberty. One morning, Mrs. L called me to the front of the class to help her hold up an illustration while she talked. I was mortified because I'd been sitting there with a hard-on that wouldn't go away. I stalled, but eventually I had to get up, much to the amusement of the class. Mrs. L later told me that if I ever felt "uncomfortable" again, I could leave the classroom until I felt better.

One afternoon, she asked me to help her make a cake for the class. We were going to have a birthday party. At her apartment in the teacherage I was standing at the kitchen counter stirring the lemon-and-sugar frosting when she stepped up behind me. "Let's see how you're doing," she said, and leaned forward, squashing her big boobs against my back. My back went ramrod straight as I tried to break contact, but she reached around and took my hands to help me stir. "Like this," she said. Then she touched me. I was too frightened and shocked to yell. I pushed her hand away and ran out the door. I hid in the trees by the trading post all afternoon. I didn't go back to the classroom, and I never told anyone.

For years, after school on Wednesday afternoons, the missionaries descended on our classrooms and we were divided up among them. This was called "religion day." Unless our parents expressly forbade our participation, it must have been assumed perfectly acceptable and part of our education. It was all for our good. This happened at school so our parents never saw what happened. The competition for bodies was fierce. Christian Reformed. Baptist. Catholic. Mormon. Presbyterian. Pentecostal. We listened to sermons and sang hymns. We could not refuse. Our only reward came at Christmas, when we got presents and small paper bags of peanuts, an orange or apple, and a handful of hard candies. The missionaries told us about heaven and hell, and they warned us about listening to false prophets. We, we were told, were heathens. I didn't know what that word meant then, but somehow I understood it was a bad thing and I felt shame. I was determined to redeem myself, however, so I sang as loud as I could and memorized endless verses and parables.

I was picked by the Christian Reformed Church to be part of their group, which was the largest. We met in the cafeteria, which doubled as the school auditorium because it had a stage. We felt proud that we were the biggest group, and we looked down our noses at the others, those "false prophets." During most of the week we children played amicably, but on Wednesday afternoons we became mortal enemies.

Mr. B, a small neat *Diné* man, would bellow "Onward, Christian Soldiers" like *bilagáanaas* did, making his voice quaver at the end of each line. We applauded the first time he did that, only to have him chastise us. He told us we should not be praising him. He was only the instrument. The praise belongs to *Him*, he said, pointing solemnly at the ceiling. He had many lessons like that. Outside of those afternoons, though, we never heard him say a word, which made his singing voice all the more startling and fascinating.

Fortunately for me and many of my classmates, at the same time that the missionaries were introducing us to their practices, we were attending our own ceremonial activities. *Ndáá'. Alch'i'niil'jeeh. Yéi'iibicheii. Dzilk'igi. Ké niiljeeh. Bijí. Azada'aníil. Názhnoodahí. 'Ootííl.*

I was initiated by my traditional grandfather into many of the ways of my people. I learned some of the prayers and songs. I learned the names of places and of the things that happened there. I learned the ceremonial names of plants, animals, and various types of earth. I learned where to find medicinal plants and how to collect them properly. I learned how to gather corn pollen. I learned many stories, and through them I learned of things that have no existence in the limited world of the *bilagáanaa*.

I saw him talk to the stars.

I was told about the power of animals and about their place in creation. I learned to sit up all night for the vigil ceremonies, and to assist him in various ways. I could help with the rituals, the preparation of certain baths, the carrying out of minor details. In learning these things, I was also learning about myself. And I received my secret, sacred *Diné* name. The name that the dieties know me by. The name used in prayers. The name that ties everything together and gives me an identity, a *presence*, in the universe.

Mom had left for church and I was alone with my brothers, Paul, who is twelve years older, and Alex, who is ten years older. The day before, they had brought back our horses from the badlands, where they had wintered. It was time to brand the new colts and fillies. Altogether we had about twenty mares with their ponies milling inside the aspen-post corral.

My brothers led me out to the corral and roped a buckskin colt. The colt was terrified and fought the rope. It reared up again and again and struck out like a maniacal boxer with its sharp hooves, but the rope only squeezed tighter each time, and the colt began to choke. Finally it stood still, its coat dark and gleaming with sweat. Then the colt's eyes rolled back in their sockets and it sank to its knees. My brother grabbed my arm and pulled me after him. He walked up to the colt and delivered a hard kick to its ribs, which brought it to its feet. It was trembling violently, almost as hard as I was, and it groaned.

"Get on," Paul said. I was scared shitless, but I was even more afraid of my brother. He would knock me around if I refused.

He hoisted me atop the colt by the seat of my pants and released the rope. The colt sprang up and danced back a few steps, then it spurted forward into the milling herd. I screamed like a girl and hung onto the colt's mane with both hands. I was crying and yelling that I was going to be killed, that I would fall off and be trampled under the churning hooves. My brothers laughed and whistled and twirled their ropes to make the horses run faster. My hands began to bleed and sting from the coarse hairs cutting into them, but I would not have let go for anything. My brothers thought it was great fun, and I think they actually thought they were doing me a favor. They thought I was being pampered too much as the youngest in the family.

After the colt had circled the corral several times, it suddenly moved to the outside of the herd and galloped alongside the posts. I saw my chance; I grabbed a fence post as we charged past it and pulled myself to safety. I jumped down the other side and ran as fast as my legs could carry me. I couldn't go back to the house, they'd only drag me back, so I ran toward a neighbor's house, hoping they'd intervene. That was a big mistake. I soon heard the sound of pounding hooves as Paul chased after me. Within seconds he crossed in front of me and cut me off, so I had to change directions. It was hopeless, but I kept running. I didn't cry, though I wanted to, because I knew it would be useless and that it would only aggravate him.

Every time I slowed, he nudged his horse against me or laid his rope on my back and legs. The fear of being trampled kept me going. He made me run in front of his horse like that until I was exhausted. By that time we were a long ways from the house, and he left me there wheezing and coughing. As much as I wanted to, I never told on them. They would give me looks when Mom came home, and I knew not to say anything. Later on, they would say something like, "He helped us with the horses." Anything I said to contradict them thereafter was futile. Mom would say, "Good, good." And that would be that.

I felt lucky they were only around during the summer. They both attended Riverside Indian School, in a far-off place called California, and for many months they were not around.

Not until many years later did I understand what BIA boarding schools were and what they had done to generations of Indian children, including my brothers. In the photographs we have from those years, their loneliness is obvious. In one, my eldest brother is outside his dormitory, holding a basketball and kneeling on an asphalt ball court. The building looms behind him, an imposing structure of red brick, all right angles, dark windows, and sharp corners. His hair is cut very short. He is smiling, squinting into the sun, but he later said that the smile was for the camera. There was a beer can by his feet, a prop that would have meant quick punishment had he been caught.

The dorm aides and teachers had absolute power. An infraction of a minor rule could result in a humiliating punishment like being forced to clean toilets with a toothbrush, or being spanked publicly no matter how old you were. Most of the Indian staff were products of the boarding school system themselves. That's all they knew. They treated you the way they themselves had been treated. They addressed you by your last name only. They could barge into your room at any time, go through your stuff, threaten demerits, withhold letters, deny telephone privileges.

But amid the horror, and against all odds, something utterly remarkable transpired—a magical flowering, if you will—an unprecedented and unanticipated development that has had repercussions all over Indian Country. When the diverse Indian nations were thrown together like that, naturally friendships, romances, and intermarriages happened. All kinds of priceless information and experience, as well as genes, were exchanged. There is a supreme irony in the fact that the government's tragic experiment in behavior modification gave birth instead to a powerful pan-Indian consciousness. Important political and social organizations resulted from that mixing of nations. "Indian Country," as we know and call it, was born.

They were gone nine months of the year, hundreds of miles to the west, at distances I could not ever have fathomed as a child. They had no choice. The whole intent was to destroy who and what they were. *Diné*. It was a new form of warfare. My eldest brother was trained to do house painting and my other brother was shunted into drafting. In one photo, Alex is standing beside the ornate stone arch at the entrance to their school, and there is a plaque set in the stonework: TRADITION IS THE ENEMY OF PROGRESS. They had only each other. They said they never cried, not even when things got so bad some kids escaped. Stories abounded about what happened to some of those runaways. Frostbite, rape, gangrene, exposure deaths.

I am not fooled. I see the suitcases sitting by the bed the moment I walk in the door. My mother is sitting at the table peeling potatoes. "Oh, you're back from school already," she tries to say nonchalantly, but her face cannot mask her happiness. I whirl, and sure enough, there they are behind the door. They are home! I stand there grinning. They grab me and tickle me and I squirm and shriek. I cannot take my eyes off them, my brothers. I trail after them everywhere they go until they tell me to leave when Ida and Mary come over. But the summer is over too soon. One day they pack their suitcases again, and then they are gone. In a month or so they will send their school pictures. Mom will buy gold frames from town and the portraits will be hung where we can see them every day.

There is another photo taken of Paul many years later. He is in Vietnam. He is outlined against a hazy sky, his skin burned a dark brown by the jungle sun. He is perched atop a stack of wooden ammo boxes. The caption printed underneath says it all: "Thinking of home."

Ahééhashiigo ninááśísdzá

(I go again to the land of everlasting summer)

At fifteen, I dropped out of high school. I decided one day that I just wouldn't go anymore. I'd had enough after a few weeks. What they were saying didn't seem in any way relevant to my life. I didn't care about the skeletal structure of bony fish or how to conjugate a verb. I wanted to know about what was *really* going on. The takeover at Wounded Knee had just happened and one windy day that spring the local chapter of the American Indian Movement took over the Fairchild semiconductor plant in Shiprock, the rez town where my high school was located.

But as the year passed from spring to autumn, I got bored and anxious staying home. The prospects of employment, slim to begin with, withered and dried up on the vine. As the days went by, I sat staring down the road. So it was a great relief when my mother showed me the letter. My uncle Ransom, whom I hadn't seen since my childhood, had written from California. She had told him about my situation. There's plenty of work down here, he said. He can stay with me until he gets on his feet.

Hell, yes, I said. I would go to Los Angeles.

There was a picture hanging on a wall in our house for many years. Ransom, young and stocky, is leaning against the hood of his shiny black Buick in front of our house, in jeans and a white T-shirt with the sleeves rolled up. A pack of cigarettes is tucked into one of the rolled-up sleeves. His hair is slicked back and there is a barely visible tattoo on one of his biceps, a souvenir from his days touring the Pacific with the U.S. Navy. We later found out he had a son in the Phillipines. In that regard, he wasn't the only one. From time to time the tribal newspaper would report on the appearance of some foreign-born person searching for their *Diné* father.

I was naive. I thought it would be easy. I thought I would save money and get rich. I would get a car, a stereo, a television. On the day I went down I still wore the reservation uniform: blue jeans, silver buckle, western shirt, and cowboy boots. I didn't realize how much I would stand out. I didn't have a clue. I was drawn by the myth. I imagined a land where the sky was always blue and the sun was always shining.

All the way to Gallup that morning I was so nervous I couldn't talk. What could I have said anyway? The mountain-tops were still mottled with snow. Auntie Mae drove me into town. All the way there, we listened to the *Diné* deejays joking. They didn't know.

Nervous?

Sure.

We'll miss you.

Me too.

Then I was alone. I checked in my baggage and sat down on the black plastic TV chair to wait. Mom had packed a lunch to eat on the bus, but I was embarassed by it—roasted mutton and green chilies, boiled potatoes and tortillas—so I ate everything inside the depot. Later, I'd have a tasteless gray meatloaf for dinner in Barstow and I wouldn't taste her cooking again for years.

When the bus suddenly appeared outside the depot in a swirl of noise and dust, a rush of fear and anxiety nearly overwhelmed me. My palms went slick with sweat. I got up and peered out the window at the two words spelling out my destination: Los Angeles. Two Indian guys got off and were greeted by relatives. *Yá'át'ééh, shiyáázh,* a woman called to them. *Yá'át'ééh nihaa nánooh t'áázh!* Then they piled into waiting cars and drove away. I took a long last look around and climbed aboard. At the top of the steps I was suddenly confronted by rows of staring *bilagáanaa* faces. I slunk into a seat next to a long-haired younger guy and busied myself settling in. He looked at me but didn't say anything. A couple hours later, at the noon stop near Houck, he got off and sat smoking on the bank of a stock pond nearby. It didn't dawn on me until later what he'd been puffing on.

Later.

"Where you goin', Chief?"

"California."

"Far out, Chief."

Being fresh off the reservation, I didn't know quite how to behave. I stepped off a curb in anticipation of a green light—

everyone did that in Gallup—and I didn't see the bus barreling down the street. A black man grabbed my shoulder and yanked me back just before the bus whooshed past. "You crazy, man?" he said. "You want to get yourself killed?"

I wandered around for hours. On Hill Street I came across a mob gathered outside a theater-cum-church, and naturally I decided to investigate. Within minutes, a buzz swept back from the front. "Here they come!" I rose on tiptoes to see who "they" were. Oh, man! I remember thinking. It was Tom Hayden and his wife, Jane. He was campaigning for some office. They were my first celebrities, so I made sure I got a good look. It helped that I was tall. The guy was rather homely, but Jane was something. The crowd dispersed rather quickly after the brief speech, and I wandered away too.

At the end of the block I looked back and saw Jane alone on the sidewalk in front of the theater. The street seemed suddenly deserted. She was standing with a child. They were holding hands, looking down the street the other way as if they were waiting for a taxi. The scene made me feel lonesome and unbearably sad.

Uncle was taking me to meet his boss the first morning. We hadn't gone too far from where he lived when I saw this woman standing on the sidewalk. She was a thin *bilagáanaa* girl with white blond hair, tight clothes, and spike heels. She was taking a deep drag on her cigarette as we passed by. She saw me looking at her and smiled. The bangle bracelets on her arm flashed when she waved. Her nails were long and red. I looked away in embarrassment. Uncle laughed. They're everywhere, he said. You'll see. In the rearview mirror, I saw her turn toward the next car and wave again.

Uncle is mean when he drinks. Our evenings revolve around championship wrestling, pints of pomegranate sloe gin, and loud arguments. The floor is a gray-and-green linoleum worn through in spots. Below Uncle's apartment is a used furniture store. The proprietors are Lorraine and George. She wears blonde Zsa Zsa wigs and faded housedresses, and his pants sag so low in back you can see the crack of his ass. Sometimes they come up to drink and play cards with Uncle in the evenings. Their daughter Cynthia has something going with Uncle, I find out. No wonder she is kind, loaning me money, making fancy casserole suppers. One morning I walk into the bathroom and there she is, flabby, naked, sitting on the bowl, smoking a cigarette and reading a magazine.

"You're fucked up, kid," Uncle says.

"Because I don't believe?"

"How blind can you be? Think about it: the earth, the sun, the whole goddamn universe. It didn't just all come out of nowhere. Somebody made them!"

"But it's not my story, shidá'í."

"You're stupid!" His fist slams onto the tabletop. The bottle jumps and tips over. "God did it!" he yells. "God!" The syrupy liquid gushes out, thick and red like blood. He backhands the bottle and sends it crashing into the wall above the stove. "Stupid—stupid—stupid!" He turns and grabs a spatula from the countertop and whacks it against the edge of the sink, chipping the enamel. I get up and back away.

At two o'clock I go into the living room and turn off the TV. He is still out, snoring on the couch, so I throw a blanket over him. "Maria, baby," he mutters. In the morning he doesn't remember anything. Eggs over easy. Burnt toast. Silence.

The bottle is gone and the shards are cleaned off the stovetop. A faint stain, a shadow of the evening, remains on the wall. He drops his plate into the sink and we leave for work.

The Fillmore Hotel is an eyesore, peeling paint and creaking floors, but it is where I live. I have moved out from Uncle's place. I am on the third floor. Roxanne and Traci, a divorcée and her teenage daughter, live on one side. On the other side is Estéban, a bachelor migrant worker who leaves buckets of whatever he's picking outside our doors, walnuts, oranges, tangerines, avocados. The walls are thin. I can hear the women arguing, screaming at each other, throwing things, throwing up. Roxy has a cigarette voice. Traci yips like a poodle. They have nightly male visitors. At Estéban's there is mariachi, corridos, and now and then, a woman, late at night, talking, giggling, crying out.

My window opens to the south, over the corrugated metal roof of the building next door. When it rains, the drops bounce off it and fill the air with mist. The sound is like sand cascading around inside a tin can. Across the street is a small palm-shaded grassy park where I hang out on my days off. My dealer knows to find me there. On the other side of the park there is a liquor store. The town has one main street, and it is backdropped by mountains that are white with snow in the winter. It is surrounded by citrus groves and eucalyptus windbreaks, both of which have a smell that burns into your memory.

I wind up working a series of dead-end jobs. It is hard at first, but I am too proud to give up. I do not want to go home in defeat, tail between my legs, so I do different things to survive.

I am a stock clerk in Franco's, a men's clothing store. The proprietor is a short nervous man with a pronounced accent, a waxed mustache, and a manicure. He is usually standing by the big window up front watching people. His name is not Franco. His words are carefully modulated; *t*'s as crisp as the tap of cymbals, *r*'s that roll off the tongue. Fr-r-ranco's.

I'm no dummy; it's obvious the moment I walk in the door. He's a sharp dresser, classy in a fussy sort of way, cool and detached. But there are moments when the façade drops, like when he is going down on his knees in front of a customer to measure an inseam, his hands trembling as he stretches the measuring tape from cuff to crotch. The customers usually pick up on the vibes and stare straight ahead, or examine the ceiling tiles intensely until he is done.

The storeroom is where he smokes and sips an occasional glass of wine. One afternoon I am in there unpacking a shipment when he comes in. He stands there motionless. I ask if there is something I can do. He shakes his head. In a few minutes, he returns. I hear his lighter click behind me. I glance back just as he is reaching. His pinkie ring glitters as hand floats through space.

There is a spark of static electricity when his hand alights on my shoulder. I flinch and he snatches his hand away. He steps back quickly and stands there blinking. I am on the edge of the chair, looking up at him. "I'm sorry," he says. "I thought . . ."

I drop the stuff I am holding. "Nope," I mumble. "No fucking way." The next day it rains and I stay home by my window all day, watching the mist churning above the tin roof.

"This soup is cold!" the old lady says. "Yes, ma'am," I tell her. I know she hasn't touched it. She and her friends have been sitting in the booth gabbing for over an hour. I take the bowl and carry it back to the kitchen. Ramón gives me a knowing look. She is a regular. She dresses well and drives a big car, but she is picky, and a non-tipper besides. The big rock on her finger could put your eye out. I zap the soup twice in the microwave. Then, after giving her back the bowl, I motion to Ramón. We hide behind the plants and watch as she scalds her mouth. She drops the spoon with a clatter and gulps some water. "Hot!" she screeches. "Waiter!"

Julian Goldstein's Egg City is three million leghorns in thirty-six open-air buildings the size of football fields. That many squawking chickens make a racket that rivals a jet engine at full throttle, and their shit has a sinus-clearing ammonia sting. Four or five birds are packed into each eighteen-by-eighteen-inch cage, and the cages are arranged into 150-foot rows. There are over 180 rows per house. In those crowded conditions the birds quickly turn psycho and begin maiming and cannibalizing each other. They flap insanely at your approach and raise a boiling white dust that coats everything. Most of them are naked because of the crowding and constant friction. There's nothing uglier than a naked chicken, believe me. Well, almost nothing. After their productivity wanes, they are sold to companies that make soups and chicken pot pies.

Most of the workers are Mexican immigrants. Agapito is my boss. He is a blue-eyed blond who owns two hotels in Mexico City. When he retires he plans to return there to lead the life of a king. When he's in a good mood you can hear him whistling or singing a long ways off. Sometimes the shop stewart would do Elvis impersonations—except for the swivel, which he said was too femmy for a Chicano man to even attempt, especially in public—for the guys gathered around the lunchwagon. The foreman, a soft-spoken Jewish guy named Sid, also a fan of the King, would politely applaud and smile.

Even the Israeli guy who hardly spoke to anyone, when he wasn't reading *Reader's Digest*, clapped and whistled.

It wasn't all roses though.

Just before I left, scores of Vietnamese refugees had begun arriving. Doctors, lawyers, university professors—whatever they had been, they were put to work feeding chickens, cleaning chicken shit, gathering and packaging eggs. They worked diligently, however, and it wasn't long before they began buying new cars. They saved money quickly because they lived in groups and shared rent and practically lived on rice. They also knew how to manage money. The guys who'd been there a while began to resent them. They began to grumble. Jealousy spread quickly. One afternoon a fight broke out in the parking lot below the office. Several Chicanos attacked the Vietnamese, but they were in for a surprise. The Vietnamese guys pulled that martial arts stuff. They fought like roosters, leaping and kicking. Needless to say, they were left alone after that.

I operated an electric feeding cart, which was a step above egg picking. But the pickers could make more money if they were fast. The cart was a metal box with two arms that lifted the feed with augers and spewed it through hoses into feed troughs as I whizzed up and down the rows. The job was dirty and monotonous and the only way to cope was to stay stoned. We smoked on the way to work, at morning break, at lunch, at afternoon break, and on the way home. Everybody did it, except maybe some of the older family guys.

One day I walked in on José fucking a chicken. I busted out laughing, it was such a ridiculous sight. Damn, I said, you'll get fired, you loco mother. You might catch some chicken disease. He only grinned and kept on loving that bird. Sometimes the birds drove you over the edge, and it was nothing to grab one from a cage and wring its neck. It would go flapping and bouncing around like it was on springs. Later, someone would sneak the carcass into a lunchbox.

Juan was my best buddy. He'd been born in Moorpark and was proud of being a U.S. citizen, but at the same time he was fiercely proud of his Mexican roots. He told me that California belonged to Mexico because the United States had illegally occupied the land. I reminded him that Mexico had taken it illegally from the Indians. His dad, Mario, worked at Egg City as a jack-of-all-trades. Juan drove trucks. The family was originally from Hermosillo. Mario put in a garden every year at an annex of the egg ranch some miles away. He also planted fruit trees, lime, avocado, pomegranate, lemon, and grapefruit.

The union was boss, and my pay and benefits were good, but one day I decided I'd had enough of the dust, the stench, the shit-streaked eggs, and the perforating noise. Where was the California that I had dreamed about? I had to find it, so I moved on to another job, and then another.

I thought I could live that way. I thought things would change. I found work and kept busy, but when I looked around one day, what I saw made my jaw drop: I was standing at a bus stop in thriftshop clothes, breathing smog, worrying about rent. For what? But I didn't act, not yet. Either I was stubborn or just plain stupid. I had to get that final kick in the gut.

"Hey, Julio!"
You talking to me?
"Yeah, you. C'mere."

I laugh out loud when he tells me what for. A big fat *bilagáanaa* in a big yellow car. I step back shaking my head, but I see the bill he wags.

"Hey kid, yes or no? I don't have all day."

I start walking. The car creeps along behind me. I hear the ticking of the engine and the tires on asphalt. I have no money. I feel like running.

"We've got to make it snappy, kid. I'm on my lunch break."

I don't say anything. Do or die. *Joto sonuvabitch!*

Later at the fast food joint, I can't even look the girl in the eye as she counts my change.

I live, but without a high school diploma, I am doomed. I know that I will always be in the same ol' boat here. Despite ambition. Despite dreams.

Tato is from Guadalajara. His English is as bad as my Spanish, but we get along. We are both young. We like to party. One night we are at a park just outside the city near the mountains. The higher peaks are luminous with snow. Down here it has been drizzling on and off for days. The stream just below the parking lot crashes over boulders big as houses. I sway in the darkness, pissing into the air from the high bank. My movements are sluggish and funny. I begin to float, and I laugh at the sudden panicky sensation of weightlessness. It occurs to me that I might jump into the water. If I do, I will bob like a cork, I think, and giggle. The thought is hilarious and I can't stop laughing. But then the rushing black water starts pulling at me. A strong wind rises up suddenly and pushes me from behind. My tongue feels like mossy stone. As I begin to sway out of control, pissing in looping arcs, Tato opens the car door and the shriek of electric guitars reach out in the rain and grab ahold of me. I hear his footsteps on the gravel and concentrate on their approach. Then I hear the soft patter of raindrops on the hood of his car. I look toward Tato, and behind him the lights of the city bloom like multicolored flowers on the horizon. Overhead, the bottom-lit storm clouds slowly drift and swirl like currents in the ocean.

Later, hanging out on Hollywood Boulevard on a Sunday, I was thrilled to see a group of Indian students walking up toward Highland Avenue. I soon realized that they were *Diné*. There was no mistaking the puffy goosedown jackets—the kind with fake fur collars in vogue then—the cowboy boots, and the silver belt buckles set with turquoise and coral.

I stayed a half-block behind them, listening to their observations and laughter. They couldn't get over the guys holding hands on the streets. Or the prostitutes who eyed and heckled them. One black girl with blond hair called them sheep. They stopped in front of a theater showing *Deep Throat* and *The Devil in Miss Jones*. The guys poked each other and pushed one another toward the door. The girls giggled and bunched together behind them. After a while, an usher came out and told them to move on.

I followed like a spy. I looked at stuff in windows. I ducked into doorways. I trailed them into a convenience store and bought gum that I didn't need. I watched them in the big round mirror. I don't know why I didn't just walk up to them.

After a while they turned onto Hollywood Boulevard and began reading the plaques set in the sidewalk. Maybe I should have showed them where John Wayne was on the Walk of Fame. No, I waited at Mann's Chinese Theater, but they didn't react like I'd expected. They only gave me a glance. For some reason, though, I was pleased. Then again, I wanted them to notice. I wanted to ask, What's going on back home? Where're you from? Look at me. But suddenly I was afraid of what they might actually say. Me in leather and my hair sprayed silver. I sensed they would not be impressed. They moved around me, intent on the footprints in the concrete. After a while, I became self-conscious standing there and eased out through the gate. Still, I lingered nearby. They left a few minutes later and walked chattering back down the street.

I returned to the reservation in April. The land was just beginning to take on a tinge of green, and the skies were bluer than I had remembered. All the way back, I tried to stay awake, not wanting to miss any part of my journey home. That is, except for the monotonous stretch of highway across the Mohave Desert, which we crossed at night, under a full moon. Even then I slept fitfully. When we crossed the Colorado River into Arizona, I woke completely. I watched the pale flat desert and the dark jagged mountains glide past. The man in the seat next to me snored softly and muttered under his breath. By four A.M. we were in Phoenix, and by sunrise we were climbing the Mogollon Rim toward Flagstaff. Then we rounded a bend and suddenly there it was, *Dook'o'oosliíd*. The San Francisco Peaks.

East of Flagstaff, the place-names danced past quickly. Meteor Crater, Joseph City, Holbrook, Winslow, Sanders, Lupton, Manuelito, Gallup.

We rolled into Gallup at eleven o'clock in the morning. Saturday is the big shopping day, and the population triples with people coming in from the surrounding reservations. On the way into town on I-40, we passed trucks packed with Indians. Their shiny pickup trucks and cars whizzed past the bus, gleaming with chrome, mufflers rumbling. Now and then, as they passed, I caught the sight of a brown face gazing back up at me. Some of the trucks carried laundry and plastic trash bags filled with crushed aluminum cans.

As we came closer to downtown, the traffic thickened and I could not take my eyes off the people. *Áhálǎanee'*. I careened between shame and pride: shame for our poverty, "dark" skin, "Indian-ness," and "primitive" ways; and pride for our resilience, our story, and our very lives. I walked slowly back down the hill from the depot. I was astounded at how old everything looked. At how small the town was. I watched the people unabashedly. The sun was bright and warm. All around me, the beautiful language rang out.

Tséhílí

(Where it flows into the canyon)

South of the Navajo Community College, where I spent a year and a half after coming back, there is a canyon and a lake above it behind a low earthen dam. The lake is relatively new and has become a magnet for fishermen from throughout the Four Corners area. Rainbow trout, which are not native thereabouts, grow to tremendous size in the cold clear water. In summer, in the fleeting shade of a passing cloud, they rise out of the water and stipple the lake surface like raindrops when they fall back. The local people don't fish there because several people have drowned in the lake since the dam was built.

The word and name *Tséhílí* refers simultaneously to the locality and the act of the creek entering the canyon there. The language is like that, full of motion. *Diné bizaad* is verb-based, whereas English is noun-based.

Tsaile is the spelling used to designate the small town that has sprung up around the college. NCC, established in 1968, is the oldest tribally controlled junior college in the United States. It is where I learned to read and write my own language. I also learned about *Diné* philosophy and art. It is where my writing career really began. Anna L. Walters, a Pawnee-Otoe woman married into our nation and an accomplished writer herself, teaches creative writing there. She was the very first person to tell me that I could write. That was a revelation. I won my first writing contest there with a tale about a young woman named Alana who saved her people from oppression by evil beings with the help of aliens stranded on her world. She overcame great perils in a fantastic journey across a dangerous continent. On the way, she was befriended and aided by an assortment of peoples including Amazons, dwarves, and beings with psychic powers. She learned to vanish at will. And she learned to fly. Unbeknownst to her she'd had those powers to begin with, but she had to discover and learn to use them.

The creek descends from the mountains rising to the east of Tsaile—the Lukachukai Mountains, a spur of the Chuskas—and tumbles from the spillway down into the canyon. This is Canyon de Chelly. *Tséghi'*, in *Diné bizaad*. The first Spanish visitors spelled *tséghi'* the way they heard it. Now it's become de Chelly, dee-shay. I had followed the stream for miles, and it seemed like a journey into another world. The silence was astounding. I heard my footsteps echo from the cliffs. Now and then I caught myself jerking my head around to catch a movement. High up on the walls were pictographs, red, yellow, turquoise, and white *Yéi'ii* figures, handprints, animals, symbols and constellations. Where water oozed out of the cliffsides in dark seams, wild grapes thrived. I touched the handprints and was shocked by the cold stone and the recognition.

At its deepest, the canyon walls rise straight up a thousand feet above the sandy floor. In cracks veining the red sandstone walls, in alcoves, on ledges, at the base of cliffs, atop rock towers, thousands of *Anaa'sází* ruins remind one and all of the antiquity of the human presence here. They are silent, but they are eloquent. Many have been plundered for artifacts, while scores of others repose in pristine condition, as if the occupants had just left for a moment and would return at any time.

My people, too, have stories about that canyon. In 1863 Kit Carson was commanded by the U.S. Army to subdue *Diné*, so he marched onto our homeland with a large force of soldiers and Indian scouts. Over the next two years he relentlessly pursued *Diné* throughout *Diné bikéyah*. Many people took refuge in the canyon, but eventually Kit Carson breached that stronghold. He carried out a "scorched earth" campaign, the systematic destruction of flocks and herds, cornfields and peach orchards, and reduced the nation to a shambles. His unrelenting campaign eventually succeeded, but while they still had the hope and the strength, *Diné* resisted. The canyon was their last refuge.

More than a century earlier, when the Spanish were doing the same thing to *Diné*, hunting them mercilessly across the rugged expanses of their homeland, one band, perhaps relatives, had sought refuge in an alcove high up in the canyon wall. They told the children to remain quiet and they might have eluded the soldiers, but a woman could not contain her anger and she stood up and screamed insults. The Spanish soldiers fired on them from the opposite side of the canyon. The bullets ricocheted off the sloping roof of the alcove and all *Diné* hiding there were killed. That alcove is now known as Massacre Cave.

A year later, I am at the University of New Mexico in Albuquerque. I have taken all the available English courses at NCC. I go to Albuquerque because Leslie Silko and Simon Ortiz are teaching there. Also because it is a city. *Bee'eldííl dahsinil*, the city named after mission bells.

Nahaghá

(The ceremony)

Until then, I hadn't mentioned the Native American Church to anyone, not even my roommate, Steve. He never would have known about it either if I hadn't slipped up. As it was, I had absentmindedly mentioned that I was going home for a visit. That's all it took. He started wondering out loud about what the rez was like. Uh-oh, I thought. It wasn't that I didn't want him to see the land and the people, but showing up unannounced with a stranger in tow that particular weekend would definitely cause a stir.

As Friday drew near, Steve began grilling me about life on the reservation. I answered honestly, but I was careful. I wanted to bore him. I was relieved when his interest seemed to wane, but the evening before I was to leave he came right out and asked. I froze, a wet plate in one hand, a soapy sponge in the

103

other, and tried to act like nothing out of the ordinary had happened.

Uncle Jim didn't have a phone, otherwise I would have had to call him right then. That would have led to a different story, believe me. I wasn't the only one uneasy about strangers. We'd seen New Agers dancing in the ruins at Chaco canyon, decking themselves out in faux Indian garb. And last summer, a bearded long-haired man had dragged a battered wooden cross into the Sundance arbor at Low Mountain.

I understood the danger. The two worlds were never meant to mix like that. Two canoes. Separate but equal. The Iroquois were right about that. How could I explain that to Steve: that we're all created different and *meant* to be that way? To have different skin tones, languages, and religions. Did the eagle try or want to be a hawk? Then again, he was someone I knew.

After agonizing over it awhile, I threw up my hands. "I guess it'll be okay, dude. It's just that—"

"Oh, cool!" He almost went through the roof. "What should I take?"

"There's something you should know," I warned. "The family's having some doings. A Scalp Ceremony. Blond locks are especially prized."

"Hey!" His blue eyes bugged out. "You're putting me on, right?"

"You have no idea what you're getting into," I told him. I realized I had a lot of educating to do. I had to spend quite a bit of time explaining what the Church was about, what would happen, and how he would be expected to behave. But he was eager. Oddly enough, I enjoyed telling once I began.

A long time ago, in a land far to the south, there was a young woman hopelessly lost in the desert. Who she was, or why she was lost, is unknown and unimportant, but what is known is that she had a vision, and that she was the recipient of a divine gift. Whatever she had been before—a woman of high status, a woman of renowned beauty, a mother, or a prostitute—she had been humbled by the ordeal. She was nothing and she was alone. She had been a long time without food or water and she was near death. On the day that she thought would be her last, she crawled under a thorn bush to await the end. She lay in the scant shade and saw death approach. In utter despair, she cried out with her last breath. To her surprise, a kind but powerful voice spoke: "Take that plant beside you and eat it. It is a gift for my red children. It is the embodiment of my love and strength." *The woman took the plant, which was Peyote, and she ate it, and she lived. It refreshed her and gave her hope. She brought that medicine home with her, and from that day forward, Azee' has been with the people.*

"Peyote?" he said. "But—"

"You can't think of it that way. This is a religious ceremony, not a drug orgy. You will sit up all night—no lying down. No unnecessary talking. You will have to wait for the intervals between song and prayer cycles to go outside. *Azee'* might cause stomach cramps, or make you nauseated. If that happens, if you throw up, most people will be sympathetic, but there are also those who will become suspicious. They will think there is something wrong. Maybe you have bad thoughts, a bad attitude, or something like that. They will think the medicine is punishing you for something. But if it gets too bad, the Road Chief and the Fire Chief will intervene. They will cleanse and restore you with cedar smoke.

"The service begins at dusk. First the smokes are prepared, a sprinkle of tobacco wrapped in cornhusks. This is to purify your thoughts and set your mind straight for the night to come. Then the opening prayer is offered and the Grandfather Peyote, which is set atop the center of the crescent-shaped altar made of tamped sand, is blessed. Then the fire is stoked and the night-long service begins. The people will sing *nahaghá biyiin*. Beautiful songs to celebrate, entreat, thank, and remember. The water drum will pass from hand to hand clockwise around the tipi. The gourd rattle, sacred staff, and feather fan will accompany the drum. The people will join in the prayers and singing and add the voices of their rattles to the music. The rattles are made of hollowed gourds filled with quartz pebbles and affixed to handles that are intricately beaded and decorated. The fans are made of hawk, eagle, flicker, pheasant, and macaw feathers, and they, too, are beaded.

"At midnight, the Road Chief will offer a prayer to mark the passage, the time of renewal, the miracle of continuity. Then the people will sing again until dawn, when the water will be brought in. This is done by a woman because women embody the generative Earth power. Everything in the ceremony is in balance. *Alkéé' sikání*, the foods-of-all-kinds, will also be brought in to nourish us and remind us of their importance, that we all spring from a common source."

We left Albuquerque right after lunch, and an hour later we passed under the bare gray peak of *Tsoodzil* near Grants. Steve was impressed with the story about the battle between the Twins and the Giant, and we stopped at the rest area so he could walk on *Yéi'iitsoh bidil*, the Giant's blood, the solidified lava flow that fills the valley below the extinct volcanic cone. He posed for pictures on the dark, frozen tide.

West of Milan and Bluewater, a curtain of red sandstone cliffs twenty miles long, one thousand feet high in places, stretched toward Gallup. "That's where the Duke himself had tea with *Diné* playing Cheyennes," I said. "In that movie, we in the audience who understood what was being said laughed ourselves silly. The 'Cheyennes' were saying, in our language, 'Come on, you cowards, let's fight. You sorry creatures crawl in your own shit like snakes!' But the bluecoat 'interpreter' told the Duke that the Cheyennes wished to live in peace with the White Eyes, his brothers, so long as the grasses grew and the waters flowed."

106

The hideous billboards east of Gallup took him by surprise: *See an Indian rug weaver. See Indian dances. Walk inside a real Indian hogan. Genuine handmade Indian jewelry. Gallup, New Mexico, Indian Capital of the World!*

Gallup is where two worlds meet, I told him, *bitsi' yishtlizhii* and *bilagáanaa*. Actually, they smash head-on. Boom! Until very recently, *bilagáanaa* and Chicano cops beat Indians over the head with blackjacks in full view of other Indians who were too scared to intervene and townfolk who just looked the other way. The jails were always full. The worst thing you could call a Chicano was "Indio." Now our votes are courted. The county sheriff, district court judge, assistant D.A., county treasurer, chairman of the county commission, seven state legislators in Santa Fe, and two in Phoenix, are *Diné*.

We left town on Highway 666, north toward the reservation. On both sides of the road new shopping plazas and stores were going up. The poorest ones around are financing this, I told him. Indian trade. Overhead, three gigantic versions of Old Glory unfurled from their masts above the American Heritage Plaza, rippling in a sudden breeze above the crowded parking lots. Sure looks like a fort, Steve said. Think about that, I said. Hitchhikers stood beside the road holding aloft brown thumbs.

Later, we topped the hill north of town and the horizon retreated thirty miles to the other side of the wide valley where White Rock and surrounding bluffs blazed with the late afternoon light. The sun was intense, slanting from the west. The flat summit of the Chuska Mountains rose to the north. Sunset would come in a couple hours and we still had sixty miles to go.

"*Níléi dzil ch'óóshgai wolyé.*"

"What?"

"That mountain's name, it means White Spruce, but of course the mapmakers spelled it wrong. *Ch'óóshgai*. That's how you say it."

An hour later we began the long, winding climb up the east side of the range. Steve kept turning around and looking back. That's way cool, man. Oh, man, look! Rainclouds on the Rockies. The valley dropping below. I had been privy to the view all my life and I could afford to keep my eyes on the pavement. Besides, over the edge the hillside plunged five hundred feet to the bottom. At Owl Springs, just below Narbona Pass, Steve insisted we stop again. We got out and hiked to the top of a nearby hill. We sat on a ledge where we could see the whole valley.

The sun was setting now, and the clouds to the east were lustrous. Gold, red, and orange. Lightning flickered within the thunderheads hanging over the Jémez and San Mateo Mountains. Alpenglow tinted the distant peaks of *Dibé ntsaa*. Nighthawks swooped. Dusk filled the valley with murky shadows, but somewhere near the center a meandering thread of water gleamed like silver. The night sky swept up from the eastern horizon and slipped overhead like a lid. The brightest stars were soon joined by a multitude.

"You are so lucky," he said.

"That's right, dude."

We finally passed the FAA installation atop the highest peak. A white geodesic dome covers the radar itself. The locals call it *Jóhonaa'éí si'á*, "the sitting Sun." That rotating dish could pick up the vibrations of a paper bag shaking in the wind fifty miles away, or so a technician had told me once. We covered the remaining two miles to Mom's place in silence. Huge pines loomed up and swept by in the glare of our headlights. Horses grazing near the road looked up and their eyes glowed fluorescent green.

My mother was the first to see us coming and hurried out to greet me, her prodigal son. Steve was completely unaware of the look that crossed her face when she leaned into the car. "Oh, you've brought a friend," she said. Nor did he notice, as he got out, the startled glances from the people gathered around the fire in front of the cabin. He smiled and nodded at them. Some of the younger people came up and introduced themselves, but the older people withdrew into silence. They watched closely. Who was this guy, and what was he doing here? But I didn't have too much time to dwell on their reaction. Mom soon had us seated at a table inside. Steve nibbled tentatively at the frybread and dipped a small spoonful of stew. He saw me watching him and blushed. I had never considered that my childhood foods, *atoo' dóó dahdíníílghaazh*, might be an acquired taste, but he wound up having two bowls.

While we were eating, someone had summoned Uncle Jim. He was suddenly there, smiling, offering his hand in greeting. Then he walked over to the cookstove. He lifted the thirty-cup coffeepot with a single hand and poured a steaming cup. Uncle Jim stood six-foot-three and weighed about 250 pounds. Steve had this look, like he was expecting him to do something. Uncle Jim picked up a teaspoon and, pinky raised, stirred sugar into his coffee. "How're you doin'?" he said.

"Okay," I said.

"Fine," Steve said.

We talked after he sat down, Uncle Jim about his day, me about school, and Steve about the trip. Every now and then I felt Uncle Jim's eyes on me. I knew he would say something. I had brought a stranger, a *bilagáanaa*, to what I understood was very sacred to him. It had never been done before, so widely known was his dislike for intruders.

Steve was oblivious to this dialogue, since it was carried on with the eyes and subtle body language. Uncle Jim was telling me that no, Steve would not be allowed to stay—much less participate in the ceremony—when Steve said, "I'm looking forward to tonight." Behind us, where other people clustered around a second table, there were murmurs. Uncle Jim smiled, but he didn't say anything. A few minutes later, he finished his coffee and stood up. "Nice to meet you," he said at the door.

I got up and followed. He must have known I'd do that because he was waiting by his truck. He was dressed in his red-and-blue NAC prayer robe. I approached nervously. I didn't know quite what to say. I knew what I had done and I couldn't justify what I was about to ask. Maybe Steve could sleep in the cabin, I said, help with firewood, or something like that. For years I had slept outside with the cooks and kids too, before I was ready to take part.

"What does he want?" he said.

"He just wants to see what it's like, I guess."

"He's not one of those *California* people is he? A New Ager?"

"No, I think he's a lapsed Catholic, actually."

Uncle Jim grinned, and his teeth gleamed like two perfect rows of white corn kernels.

The fire inside the tipi was lit, and it began to glow from within. The Fire Chief and Uncle Jim's assistant were silhouetted on the stretched canvas, moving here and there. A few latecomers arrived and were ushered into the cabin to eat first. The drummer tried out the water drum, changing the tone and pitch as he swirled the water inside and adjusted the buckskin top. Steve stood by the fire outside Mom's cabin watching the people begin entering the tipi. I felt bad, but I also understood Uncle Jim.

"You know I don't condone this kind of thing," he said. "But I suppose you'll need him to help drive back tomorrow."

I nodded.

"I'm sure his help will be much appreciated by your mother too," he added.

I knew that was the best I could expect. He had every right to ask an outsider to leave. I knew it was difficult for outsiders to understand, but if they respected us they would accept this way we had. It was not an easy decision. Another uncle had refused to perform a Blessingway for one of my nephews because his mother was *bilagáanaa*. That made him *bilagáanaa* too, since we inherit our mother's clan. That was the problem. If the ceremony was done for him, that would set a precedent. These ceremonies were given to us by the Holy People at the time of the Emergence, when they taught us the proper way to invoke their aid through the prayers, songs, and rituals they contain. They would respond to whoever offered these songs and prayers. If they were used by or on behalf of *bilagáanaas*, the Holy People would respond to them too. It would become holy for them as well—or perhaps, instead. *Jóóbiida bá didooyiil*, he had said. There was a very real possibility that we would lose everything if that happened. They would possess our ceremonies then. The Holy People would know them and they would have access to the power of the Holy People. The Holy People are capable of both good and evil and they would fulfill any prayer, any wish, if the ceremony was done right. That was the danger. What if they were used against us?

I understood Uncle Jim and I knew the iron strength of his will. The decision was more than fair. I turned and waved at Steve, who quickly walked over. Uncle Jim nodded. "You got yourself a lawyer here," he said, "who just got you put on probation." He paused just before he reached the entrance and called me over. "You too," he said, motioning to Steve.

We followed soundlessly on the grass.

"The tipi is a living thing, not just wood and canvas. We must be thankful for the shelter it gives and the lessons it offers," Uncle Jim explained as we walked clockwise around it, touching the posts. Then we went inside and walked clockwise around the altar and the fire. The people murmured greetings. Just before we went back out, the Fire Chief threw a pinch of cedar on the coals and I showed Steve how to bathe himself with the fragrant white smoke.

I wonder what he'll tell his friends in California, I thought. How do you explain something like this? How do you compare this to anything in his world? Steve stood gazing into the fire for a moment, and I thought I saw his lips move.

We stood by the fire outside the cabin for a while before I left to join the others in the tipi. Later, I could hear his voice outside, above the crackle of the fire, talking to the children. He slept in his car, though Mom had offered him a bed inside. "No, I want to see the stars, and I want to watch the goings-on," he told her. "I want to hear the singing and drumming, and I want to see the dawn come."

Ootííl

(It is being carried)

One afternoon that same summer, I decided to
take a break from school and drive home from Albuquerque
for a couple days. North of Gallup, just past the reservation
hamlet of Tohatchi, I came across an interesting sight; five or
six cars, a U-Haul truck, and a Winnebago, pulled off the road.
The occupants were standing along the barbwire fence that
marks the highway right-of-way, watching a group of thirty or
forty *Diné* riding past on horseback.

The man in front, the man carrying the ceremonial wand, is riding
a palomino. The horse is outfitted with the finest fittings the man
owns, silver-decorated bridle flashing in the sun, expensive saddle
gleaming, the colorful fringe of his handwoven saddle blanket bobbing
like a deer's tail to the rhythm of the horse's movement. The man

113

sits erect, attentive but relaxed, one hand clasping the reins while the other rests lightly on his thigh. He is dressed in a dark green velveteen shirt, blue jeans and moccasins, and a silver concho belt that shoots splinters of light. A red handkerchief tied in a headband holds his black hair in place. The rest of the men follow, dark faces intent on the ride, moving together like a single body, horses bobbing through the grass and heat, manes and tails trailing out like flags. There are stocky quarter horses, beautifully spotted Appaloosas, buckskins, roans, sorrels, an albino, a pinto, and a black horse whose coat gleams like oil. The younger men crowd the man in front, eager for the ride, while the older men bring up the rear at a more leisurely pace. Some of the young men are dressed in fancy western attire, bright shirts and fancy boots, while others wear long hair, T-shirts, and hightops. The older men are in western shirts and jeans, boots and cowboy hats. Except for the pounding hooves, they are silent.

The men were engaged in what we call *Ootííl*, a part of *Ndáá*, the Enemyway ceremony. On the third night of the four-day ceremony the sponsor—or patient, as the person for whom the ceremony is being held is called—conveys by horseback to the homestead of a second person, someone who's had the ceremony done for him or her, a decorated juniper wand topped with sprigs of greenery and wrapped with lengths of colorful yarn. Horsemen accompany this person throughout. This can produce quite a sight, as the motorists had discovered.

I pulled over and walked up to the *bilagáanaas*. "Howdy," said a tall man in mirrored sunglasses. "You from around here? What's going on?"

"War party," I said. A woman whom I took to be his wife had come up beside him. She clasped his elbow.

"What?" she said.

"Heh-heh," he said, casting a glance toward the horsemen. "Sure movin' fast, ain't they?" They were now at a distance, heading south, moving along at a fast clip.

114

"They must be mad at somebody," I said. "Sometimes them traders pull a fast one. Get these people riled up."

"But, this is the twentieth century!" blurted the wife.

"A pissed-off bunch of Navajos know no bounds," I told her. "They once hunted down a trader and staked him to an anthill for cheating them out of their welfare checks."

The man looked at his wife. She looked at me. *Welfare.* The word hung like a barbed thing between us.

Just then the rest of the ceremonial entourage drove by on the highway, a line of about thirty or forty cars and pickup trucks towing horse trailers, their radio antennas and door mirrors decorated with bright skeins of yarn fluttering in the wind. They had dropped off the riders somewhere further back and were now heading up the road to a point where they would meet them. In the old days these rides sometimes took all day, but now people haul their mounts part of the way. This is partly because people work nowadays and can't get time off to ride all day. Also, though no one would admit to it, these guys aren't as tough as our ancestors were. You can't spend all week being a desk jockey, frying burgers, silversmithing, or lying on your back fixing cars, then jump on a horse for a long galloping ride. Neither the horse nor the rider could hack it. That's the bottom line. The next best thing is to make things practical.

"Just kidding, folks," I said. They seemed a bit flustered at first, but then we started talking. I told them what really was going on. They were surprised that we still carried on our ceremonies.

"*Our* Indians back east have lost their culture," said the woman. "You can't always tell who's Indian anymore."

The man seemed embarrassed by her remark. He looked for a moment in the direction the men had gone, then he held out his hand. The wife had returned to their car. A slight breeze ruffled the thin hair on his head. One after another the other vehicles pulled back onto the highway and sped away.

"I wish I knew more about this," he said, gesturing vaguely around. "It's so beautiful." Then he gave me his card, saying he'd like it if I kept in touch.

Na'nízhoozhí

(Where the bridge crosses)

The streets and alleys of *Na'nízhoozhí* were my daily stomping grounds for nearly two years after my departure from the UNM in Albuquerque, where I'd dropped out after a year of booze and bad grades. The ensuing downward spiral led me to Gallup, where my days became a blur of alcohol and living day to day. It turned out to be among the most challenging and humbling of times I've known. I saw the depths to which I am capable of descending, and that has made me stronger. I made friends with numerous people, many of whom are now dead. I saw human frailty and dignity—*human life*—laid bare. I also fell in love and was loved in return. With no concern with materiality, that is the purest love I've ever known, but my love soon died and no one has even come close since.

117

The room is perhaps fifty by fifty feet, with a cement floor and painted cinderblock walls. There are approximately one hundred men in the cell tonight. It is just after closing time and the Protective Custody vans bring in load after load of men and women. The women are taken to their own section of the jail and they can be heard talking and laughing.

There is a long metal bench encircling the cell. The earlier arrivals have already staked out spots on the bench and the latecomers curl up on the floor. The naked lightbulbs in the ceiling glow brightly all night. The men talk and laugh. There are two toilets, stainless steel, out in the open, with a small sink attached to each. A thin stream of liquid trickles from the base of one and runs into the drain hole at the middle of the floor. Some of the men are so out of it that they don't know they're sprawled in dirty water. In time, everyone has found a spot to lie down, and the floor is a carpet of closely fitted bodies. Snores fill the room. Someone curses at a pickpocket.

I wake sometime in the night. There is Sammy in one corner, with his permed hair, gold lamé top, and tight black pants. His face is garishly made-up. He is talking with some guys. He and his friends are well known and generally respected in town, except by non-Indians, who often jeer and swear at him. Sammy is a brawler, despite his effeminate appearance and mannerisms. He is left alone pretty much because people know that he will fight like a cornered dog, and that others will help him. But this doesn't mean things are always fine. Within the two years I was living the street life, three of Sammy's friends were brutally murdered. One was set afire and left smoldering at the city dump.

It is cold and I am curled into a tight ball inside my coat. I am lying under a thin sheet of plastic in a weedy ditch next to an automobile dealership. Though it is freezing and the weeds are covered with frost, I have managed to get some sleep. I vaguely remember being at the American Bar. I remember dancing, and then Liz asking me to go home with her. Why am I here? I'll wait awhile longer, then get up before the PC vans start patrolling. They usually check the ditches and alleys, looking for exposure victims. I am lucky. I know this is stupid, sleeping in the weeds in the dead of winter, but what can I do? I don't want to go home.

I get up after a while, wash up in a restaurant bathroom and walk slowly back downtown. Halfway there, someone recognizes me and pulls over. "*Ti'l!*" they say, and away we go. I don't think about where I'll wind up. There is pot and booze. Besides, they are thinking of getting a room. We cruise around a bit, stopping here and there to talk to the people on the streets, trying to pick up women. Eventually we talk two into coming with us and we drive to the Rodeway Inn.

The women are soon drunk and the guys connive to get them into the sauna, where they wilt in the heat. Later, they pass out in the room. The guys pull their pants and panties off and mount, drunk as they are. I turn on the television and watch Lassie. You're next, says one later, rising up on his elbows from the far bed. No, thanks, I tell him, and put her pants back on for chrissake. Lame dick, he says, wimp. He rolls over and soon he is snoring like a buzzsaw. The other guy gives up and passes out too, sprawled atop the red-haired woman. I take a shower and wipe the worst stains from my clothes. I don't look half bad, I think, ignoring my bloodshot eyes and shaking hands.

They wake after a couple of hours and the women stumble out the door bleary-eyed and angry. How would you like it if someone did this to your mother or sister? says the red-haired one. Our mothers and sisters are at home where they belong,

119

says one of the guys. Assholes, says the other woman, and slams the door.

I don't know where I lost them. All of a sudden I am in the back of the PC van, bouncing around as the driver curses and speeds down the alleys after running drunks. There are others in the van and they yell and cheer the chase.

Jimmy and I are coming back with a twelve-pack from Paramount Liquors. He is ahead of me on the narrow trail snaking through the tall weeds. Suddenly he jerks to a stop and I bump into him. He shakes his head and points. There, at the bottom of the ditch where we'd been planning to drink, is someone's brown ass rising and falling. They are facing away from us, their faces hidden behind a clump of weeds. They don't see us. "Shit," says Jimmy. "Some people don't got no shame." He rattles the paper sack and the man stops and looks over his shoulder at us. He grins, like it's the most normal thing in the world—outdoors, in broad daylight.

"What're you doing?" says Jimmy.

"Making love," says the man.

I'm so hungry my stomach feels like it's being squeezed in a vise. I don't remember the last time I ate. The sisters at the mission have banished me from their feeding station because they think I'm selling drugs. I can't donate at the plasma center. There are no aluminum cans to be found anywhere. So I wander the streets, looking for someone I know. There's no guarantee. You think you know someone, but they can turn on you, tell you to beat it. Or they say, what're you doing here if you're so hungry? Go home.

I am walking down the street when I notice the big car go by. It slows down and pulls over. The driver flashes the brake lights. I look around. There's no one else about. I walk up slowly, trying to look cool. The windows are tinted, so I can't see inside. I only see my grim-looking self reflected in the window. Then the dark glass hums open. Electric windows.

Oh, it's you, I say. New car, huh?

We are sitting under the shade of a big piñon tree above Washington Park. There is a softball game in progress. A young Chicano couple, kids actually, are making out in the parking lot. "Hoo-boy," says Mike, "look at 'er suck lip."

"A pro," says Dave.

"You guys," says Melanie. She looks at me. Her eyes are light brown.

It is a hot day, blue sky with just a few clouds floating overhead. To the east, *Tsoodzil* is shrouded in dark clouds and rain. Two suitcases of beer sit in the shade with us. Empty cans litter the brush. Dave passes a joint. Cheers rise from below. Cars honk. The people on the bleachers rise and whistle as a chubby woman scurries home. The outfielder is climbing over the fence to get the ball. "Look at that cow hoof it," says Mike.

We laugh.

Andalé, Mike shouts.

Melanie looks away.

An hour later, he is passed out. Melanie is making out with Dave, Mike's friend, and I'm still not drunk. I open another beer and watch the rain approach. Thunder rumbles. Dave and Melanie move away, over the side of the hill. "Don't look," says Dave.

They are gone for a long time. Finally, I get up. What am I waiting for? They ain't coming back for nothing. I damn sure wouldn't.

Take your time, Dave.

Life is short, Melanie.

I take a twelve-pack and walk down the hill to the ballpark. I sit in the dugout and wait. In a few minutes, big drops begin to pound the dirt powdered up by the ball players. Little puffs of dust rise in clouds from the force of the drops. Soon, a curtain of cold water closes over the valley. I see Mike sit up and wipe the rain from his face. He looks around. He moves deeper under the sheltering branches, walking on his knees, a twelve-pack clutched under each arm. *I once saw a bear carry two sheep like that.* Dave and Melanie walk by, heads down, sliding and staggering in the mud.

I light a joint and open another beer. I love summer thunderstorms.

I am walking along. Someone calls my name. I look up. It's Billy. "Hey, Billy!" I wave. He starts across the street, but he falls halfway. I look at him lying there. I think he's going to get up. But he doesn't. He starts to shake and stuff comes out of his mouth. A huge truck with mud-bogger tires screeches to a stop, inches from his head. "Son of a bitch!" says the driver. He gets down and pulls Billy off the street. "Goddamn drunks! Why don't you all die?" I look at him. A *bilagáanaa* with a beard. He spits at me. The spit, white and foamy, lands on my shoe. Billy moans. He is grinding his teeth. I don't know what to do. A *bilagáanaa* woman runs out from a store. She kneels beside him and sticks a pencil between his teeth. Another woman calls from the doorway. "The cops are on their way, Flo."

My eyes are almost swollen shut and my lips feel like sandbags. One sleeve is ripped off and the broken threads circle my arm like fringe. My right leg feels hot. The pain comes in waves. I hobble down the alley. I cannot bring myself to walk out into the open. Instead, I sit down on a small platform—a loading dock—and just sit. I keep spitting blood and I move my tongue around my mouth feeling for loose teeth. Luckily, they are all sound. My nose throbs. My vision blurs and for a brief moment I panic at the possibility of blindness. My sore ribs make breathing difficult. I feel so stupid. I should have known better than to deal with them. What was it, three—four guys? One holding me from behind, for sure. Fists jack-hammering my gut, and when I'm on the ground, gasping and trying to cover my head, rapid-fire kicks with pointy-toed boots. Spanish words and laughter. My buckle snapped off my belt, my boots, my wallet. Fuckin' wetbacks! But they laugh and run down the alley. Suddenly I retch and everything goes black.

I sit there in the alley until dark. People pass by and look at me. The fingernail on my right pinkie is missing. It is a bloody stub, pulsing with pain. I cannot cry, I cannot curse, I cannot walk. Evening comes and the streetlights begin to glow. Only then do I struggle up, lean against a dumpster. I have pissed my pants. I find my wallet not far away, the papers and pictures scattered down the block. I collect the things slowly. Sarah. Dark eyes. A nice smile. What should I do?

She is tiny and I feel clumsy—too large, like a bear. Her hair is spread out. So beautiful like that. Without warning, she slides a finger between my asscheeks. Don't. I pull her hand away. She laughs. Prude, she says. I don't like it, I tell her. She sighs and taps her nails against my back. Then she brings a hand around, pinches my left nipple. Don't. Her hand drops to the sheets. She goes completely limp. The moment is spoiled. I look down at her. I can't tell what she's thinking. Ah, shit, that's it—game's over. I stare at the ceiling. What's wrong, what's with you? I light a cigarette. It's not me, she says, it's you, you're too damn *predictable*, I want something different. Different, I say, that's a good one. I try to laugh. She smiles. I want to hit her. Instead, I get up and get dressed.

It's pathetic, I know.

She is sweet when she wants to be, but when she's in a bad mood like this . . . I should have expected it, though. It's how we got together. I feel her words lodge like a rock in my gut. "Where are you going, hon?" she says. It is not a question.

We met through a former buddy. He brought her back to the motel after closing time. He had gone back to the bars after I passed out. I woke to her shaking my foot. Hey you, she said, what's your name? I don't remember what happened next, exactly, but somehow she talked me into it. She liked two guys at once. I had never done that before, and I never did it again. I should have stopped then, but with someone like her you don't think with your head. I saw her every chance I got.

Now here we are. Her still in bed, smiling so sweet, and my hand is reaching for the door.

What makes an otherwise sane and humble man behave like a child? It has something to do with thinking too much, I suppose, and seeing and knowing too much. And fear. I am afraid to face my own life. I am Indian. I am minority. I am dark and I am powerless. The only way to cope is to numb the senses, to blot out chunks of time so they pass quickly. Others have other reasons. I know stories about bad luck. I've heard plenty.

One day around noon, I am walking along with Loren when he says, let's go to the soup line. The mission is on the north side, on the wrong side of the embankment carrying Interstate 40 through Gallup. The twenty-foot-high embankment built during the mid-eighties inspired a lot of jokes because it cut straight through the center of town like a medieval wall, separating the poor black and Chicano neighborhoods on the north side from the wealthy *bilagáanaa* neighborhoods on the southside.

We go our usual route down Coal and 66 Avenue ("Get your kicks on Route 66") with their clutter of tourist traps, greasy spoons, and pawnshops; across the Third Street bridge, the steel-and-concrete span that shelters a favorite party spot; and then up Maloney toward the mission. But something is going on. There are cars everywhere, swarms of people not usually in the neighborhood. We look at each other. "Hey, what's happening, man?" we ask a woman coming our way.

"I dunno," she says. "Maybe somebody's hurt. Maybe there was a fight."

We get to the mission and there are people all over the place. We don't read the papers so we don't know what's going on. Neither do most of the people gathered around. We are too shy to ask the *bilagáanaas* standing off to one side. We are filthy compared to them and I am too embarrassed to approach. *Excuse me, sir. Would you happen to know what all the commotion is about?* No, sir, they'd wrinkle their nose and tell me to go away. So we resort to jokes.

"Maybe its the pope."

"I say it's Geraldo."

Suddenly there are sirens. A motorcade approaches and creeps up Fifth Street toward the mission. Two cops on motorbikes herd people off the streets. We are pushed to one side and we crowd up against the mission walls. The silent nuns in blue-and-white habits cluster in our midst, smiling, clasping their hands. They look so happy. This must be something special,

125

I think, maybe it *is* the Pope. The first car stops and nothing happens for a moment. Then the door is opened and the crowd surges forward. I don't see anyone get out, but the people up front carry on like Jesus himself has arrived. I hear sobs, I see people cross themselves, and I feel something ripple through our massed bodies.

Then I hear the name: *Mother Teresa*. The mission is run by the Little Sisters of the Poor. She is tiny, but there is something powerful about her. She reminds me of our own matriarchs, and her kind eyes make me feel as if she *understands*. She talks to the people who crowd around her. One man, obviously drunk, drops to his knees in front of her. He is crying. "I love Jesus," he says. She touches the top of his head and I want to cry too. I am surprised by my emotions, confused. Is this a sign that we're not alone after all? That our suffering is not in vain? But how long? How much more?

The reporters, politicians, and city brass wait for her near their vehicles. They are surrounded by filth. I can see it in their eyes. They are reluctant to come close. They wait for her to come to them, but she doesn't. She doesn't see them. She stays with us for some time, talking, touching people. She tells us not to give up. *Do not give up hope.* She is so small, she cannot be seen above the greasy heads of hair. She is dark, like us. Her eyes remind me of my grandmother.

Harvey wipes his mouth with the back of his hand after he chugs heartily from the quart. He is in his Rambo outfit, camouflage pants and black T-shirt. We are sitting in the shadow of a row of poplars, leaning against a chain-link fence separating the asphalt basketball court from the alley. The blacktop in front of us is striped with long tree shadows and orange light coming from the street lamps hanging over the alley. The buildings on either side of the court—a fire station

126

and tire store—are dark. I imagine the firemen upstairs twisted up in their sheets, muscles tensed in anticipation of the next shrill alarm. The quart is cold in my hands but I sip half-heartedly. I don't know what's wrong. I just don't feel like it this evening even though it's Saturday.

Traffic drones on Maloney and the air is heavy with the noise of the weekend crowd.

"I wasn't sure at first," Harvey says. "And I don't know what told me, see? You know how that goes. Anyways, we was standing there passin' around the Mad Dog when he walked outta the alley, soundless as a cat. We're all fucked up an' we pass him the bottle without thinkin'. Later on, he pulls out a bottle and we finish that too. But there's somethin' buggin' me. You know that feelin' when somethin's not right? There's somethin' 'bout this guy, I think. He doesn't say nothin'. He's too quiet. That's when it hits me. 'Member what they say about this place, all the bad things that happen, all the partyin' and bad stuff goin' on? That's why those kind of people come here. If they *are* people, that is. So I check 'im out. I see that he's lookin' at me and he's grinnin' real wide, like he knows what I'm thinkin'. Shit, them chills run up my spine like ice water! I knew it for sure then. I wanted to yell and get away, but I couldn't move! I was frozen. I thought I was a goner, man, till I finally 'membered what Milton said one time. So I tried to wiggle my little toe. When it moved, my breath comes out in a whoosh. *'Get outta here,'* I yell, *'I know what you are!'* The guys stopped their jabberin' and stood there with their mouths hangin' open. Then that guy started laughin' real scary-like an' we all hightailed it, bumping and scraping down the alley."

There is a small village and shopping plaza north of Gallup, the Navajo Shopping Center. The grocery store there sold cheap booze, mainly fortified wines, which appealed to the down-and-out, and it was a notorious drinking spot until very recently. Panhandlers wandered the parking lot begging change. Now and then one would crawl under a vehicle to sleep it off and get run over. In winter, the bare cold sky would be laced with streamers of smoke coming from fires built to keep warm in the fields and hills surrounding the place.

Low ridges shelter the village and shopping center to the north and west. Just to the south is the rusting remains of a small power plant once fueled by local coal mines. The smokestack is visible for miles around. *Ligaii yaa'á*, "white standing up," is what *Diné* call this place. All around it and the shopping center are fields of sagebrush, harboring intricate networks of trails and clearings used as living quarters and party spots. Each winter the county police harvest frozen bodies from these fields.

One day, coming into town with my brother—I'd gone home for a respite—I saw a couple of police cruisers and a fire truck parked by one of these fields. For some reason I felt my skin crawl. A part of the field had been reduced to smoking ash.

The following day, I heard the story.

There was a woman known as Long Tall Sally. She had a high forehead and thinning hair. She'd been at a party in the sagebrush with her friends and somehow the fire they built to keep warm got out of control. With a sudden wind fanning it, the fire roared through the field in minutes, cutting a long black swath through the gray shrubs. All the others managed to escape the inferno, drunk as they were. The story is that she became disoriented and ran back into the flames. There was endless speculation about that—about whether she did or didn't know what she was doing. Everyone agreed, however, that her cries were terrifying.

In the time that I was living the street life, I saw many of my friends die. I saw their noses collapse against their faces, nostrils squashed flat, tips shot through with veins. I saw their chests swell up with cirrhosis. I saw their lips become loose. Mouths gap-toothed. And worst of all, I saw their eyes turn yellow, glassy and unfocused. Although I survived those years, I know that in many ways I never left that place. There is something about knowing it is always so near, and that being an Indian in America will make the difference.

Shilíi

(My horse)

One warm sunny day in the spring, I saddle up my horse, Ace, and head up the mountain. Some of our cattle have wandered up early and I have to check on them. They are still calving and we can't afford to lose any. The October cattle auction provides a big part of our yearly income. Without that extra cash, the kids wouldn't get enough school clothes. But truthfully, that is not the main reason I go. The mountains are a part of my identity, and my first ride to the summit each spring is a confirmation.

The foothills are a half-mile west of my house, a leisurely five-minute ride. If in a hurry though, Ace—who is a quarter horse—can cover the distance in no time flat. I'd hunker down and lean forward in the saddle to reduce drag, and we'd fly. But today we are in no hurry.

131

Ace knows where we are going, and he is eager. We set off and quickly scale the first hill, which rises a couple hundred feet above the plain. Thereafter, the mountains rise and rise. The foothills are deeply eroded and rocky. There isn't much vegetation and there is nothing to hold the soil except rock. For a while we clatter up the slopes, keeping a sharp eye out for rattlesnakes. Most of the time they'll remain completely motionless and you'd never know they were there. Sometimes, however, they are in a mood.

The beds of clay and shale underlying the mountains rise in gray, yellow, tan, and white hummocks and tiers all around us. Pygmy junipers dot the hills like cloves on a ham. Here and there spikes of waxy white-and-yellow yucca blossoms stand out against the background of brown rock. Tiny red jewel-like flowers, among the most beautiful I've ever seen, and which appear only briefly in the spring, fill crevices and ledges. Silverleaf nettles colonize the hollows. Gleaming flakes of mica and petrified wood litter the flats. Now and then we come across an abandoned campsite, and the mind creates stories to fit them. Circular arrangements of rock dating back who knows how long?

Slowly, the vegetation changes as we gain altitude. Piñon forests appear and thicken. High above, on the rim of the summit, individual ponderosa pines are outlined against the sky. A hawk circles overhead in the rising thermals. Jays scold and chipmunks chatter from atop lichen-covered boulders. A mountain bluebird flashes brilliantly in a meadow. There is the pungent scent of sagebrush and the unforgettable sweetness of cliff roses.

Before long, we reach the springs. I get down on my knees and drink directly from the pool of cold water bubbling from underground. It tastes faintly of roots and earth. When I linger too long, Ace nuzzles me aside for his share. He drinks with loud sucking noises. Then he sighs contentedly and leans his enormous weight against me. "*Nídaaz yee' héi, ashkii,*" I tell him. The saddle leather creaks. I fill my canteen and we continue.

We stop for lunch at my family's other camp, the one midway between the summit and the flats. A small boy and girl are playing in an oak nearby, and they watch me. Their flock grazes in our empty cornfield. I call the kids over and they come shyly. I give them my can of soda and they giggle. A couple of dogs are with them and they stare at me as I eat. The little boy shares a piece of my cold chicken with his sister and they throw the bones to the dogs. His name is Ambrose and hers is Carrie. I know their parents. I used to play with them in that same tree. In a while, the sheep gather together. They slip under the barbwire fence one by one and set off for home in single file, their heads down, bellies heaving like bellows. The children follow them, stopping now and then to investigate something, a bug, a plant, a small animal.

Over the hill are the neighbor's cornfields. They are green with thousands of tiny shoots. I ride along, watching the rows slip hypnotically past, and I don't see that the sweat lodge at the other side of the field is in use. There is a shout and I stop. Someone waves. I squint, trying to make out who it is. "*Hágoh!*" says the figure, and I recognize the voice. It is the children's father. I go over and tie Ace to a juniper, but he doesn't like that, so I free him and he immediately begins to graze.

Jim has cleaned out the sweat lodge and there is a heap of ferns waiting to be arranged inside. A fire of pitchwood roars, heating the pile of lava rock set underneath. Jim invites me to join him, and since I'm in no hurry, I accept. Ever since my grandfather died years before, there has been no one to sweat with, and it doesn't feel the same alone.

The air is motionless in that secluded spot, and the sun is warm on my bare skin. This is freedom. We are surrounded by silence, leaves, and shadows.

We arrange the ferns, and after Jim stacks the hot rocks inside, we enter and close the flap. We sweat for what seems like hours, but I know it is really only a matter of minutes. Then we emerge into the cool air after four sweats and splash in the nearby pond. Going from hot to cold like that is unforgettable. Nothing will give you a greater sense of clean.

When I was a child, our city-raised cousins came to visit one summer, and as he did every week, Grandpa prepared the sweat bath. They wanted to take part and they followed us. At the lodge, Grandpa tore strips of cloth off a rag and passed them around. Our city cousins were puzzled. Grandpa had to explain: You tie it here, like this. But they were circumcised. They pinched and pulled to no avail. We fell all over each other laughing. Our cousins were embarrassed and started crying. But that did no good. Grandpa was strict about the rules. The ties served a purpose, both practical and symbolic. Given the heat, any odor in the sweat lodge will be intensified and induce headaches or nausea, and that would interrupt the sweat and defile the ceremony. You also risked sterility. The other reason was that symbolically it kept the sweat lodge holy by closing off the baser things associated with maleness. But not everything was somber. My cousin would piss with the tie still on and his dick would puff up like a water balloon.

After dressing and thanking my host, Ace and I continued up the trail. The crowns of ponderosa pines rose higher and higher, and lush glades of ferns appeared underneath the oak groves. Thick layers of dry leaves rustled under Ace's hooves. Brilliant blue lupine and red Indian paintbrush mottled the dense green meadows. The air grew cooler and we passed through the forest on a bed of pine needles. Ace was the kind of horse that hardly ever startled, and a good thing too, since now and then a wild turkey or deer would burst unexpectedly out of the dense foliage. Ace would only swivel his ears forward and look. At the foot of the escarpment lifting the summit high above us, the forest became even more dense. Spruce and aspen mingled with the pines and oak.

134

The final ascent to the top is as difficult as it is spectacular. The trail is narrow and there are numerous switchbacks. The angle is so steep, I have to get off and walk ahead of Ace. He scrambles after me, scattering rocks off the trail into the foliage clinging to the slope. The plants swish and rustle for long moments until the rocks stop far below.

Hazy blue mountain ranges hem the edge of the world. The valley is an enormous tan and pale green bowl. The village is a sparkling smudge near the wrinkled foothills. Tiny antlike trucks mark the path of the highway winding along the base of the mountains. To the south, rain clouds are approaching.

I usually saddle up every other day when I'm not busy and check on the cattle. It is both a chore and a pleasure. I can disappear into the forest and emerge somewhere else, someplace where I can believe it is a hundred years ago or even further back. Except for contrails overhead, there is nothing to show the year. The forest is timeless. I follow a stream for miles, listening to the water. The whole summit is tilted slightly to the west, and runoff pours over the western edge in waterfalls, or in numerous streams that have carved deep canyons into the layers of rock that compose the range. They are shady and filled with trees. Eagles nest in the rocky cliffs, and hawks fight with ravens over territory among the pines. Deer are content and fat. The smell of damp earth is heavy in the canyons, ripe with the smell of rotting wood and leaves. Ridgetop trees are stunted and twisted from the battering winds and the thin air. Some of the trees at the bottom of the canyons are giants, four feet in diameter, over one hundred feet tall, and hundreds of years old. There, in the absolute stillness, I can believe there is no Kit Carson. No Niña, Pinta, or Santa Maria.

Our mountain homestead is located in a valley about two miles south of *Bééshlichíi'ii bigiizh* and the FAA radar. The road passes right through the center of this clearing, and our cabin sits off to one side, behind a thicket of young pines. There is a ridge covered with aspens to the east, and from there the land slopes down toward the west. The clearing once hosted several *Ndáá'* each summer, but eventually the site was abandoned and for several years the ceremonial structures, *chaha'ooh*, sat empty.

Most people move down from the mountains in late August when school starts because children are the main caretakers of livestock during the summer, but my mother stayed until the aspens turned gold and the grasses began to dry up. Often she would be the only one up there. She kept busy and didn't miss company, she said, but one year company appeared unexpectedly.

One morning while she was out gathering kindling for a fire to make breakfast, she saw a young *bilagáanaa* woman walking up the road. This wouldn't be so unusual in the middle of summer—we get all kinds of people passing through then— but the woman had ventured up there after all the other people had left. The mountains were so quiet. The woman saw my mother and stopped by. My mother told her that everyone had left and that they were alone. The woman did not appear concerned. She said she was traveling around the country seeing places, and she didn't want to be around crowds anyway.

My mother described this woman as a "hippie." My mother said: "She wore a T-shirt with no bra and this skirt that looked like she had cut up some old jeans and sewed them back together." She carried only a backpack and canteen. The woman decided to set up camp nearby in one of the vacant ceremonial *chaha'ooh*. She slept under the stars at night and visited my mother every day. They would have tea and lunch together. The woman asked a lot of questions, my mother said, but they got along. "She poked around in the woods most of the time, but at noon there she would be, with her tea bag and that sack of peanuts and raisins that she ate."

Whoever she is and wherever she is now, that woman has some of my mother's stories, as well as this story: One night, sometime after midnight, this woman came banging on my mother's door. My mother said she was startled out of a sound sleep. It took her a while to realize who it was. The woman sounded hysterical. My mother thought the woman had been visited by a bear—she'd warned her about sleeping out in the open, alone like that—but what had frightened the woman was something else altogether.

"I opened the door and that girl nearly yanked my arm off, pulling me outside," my mother said. The woman was incoherent and frantic and kept gesturing at the sky. So my mother looked. There was a luminous orb drifting high over the clearing. Strange as it was, my mother had seen it before. "Sometimes, when I went out late at night, there it would be—just like the full moon," she said. "It came only after everyone had moved back down."

The *bilagáanaa* woman was nearly in a frenzy, but my mother didn't know what to say. "What could I do, lie to her? Tell her it was Indian magic? I didn't know what the thing was either," she said. They watched the thing until it moved out of sight behind some pines. The woman didn't go back to her camp until sunrise. That day my mother waited for the woman, but she didn't show up. My mother walked over to the *chaha'ooh* to check on her, but there was no one there.

Apparently, the woman had been lying there looking up at the stars when she saw the thing appear out of the stars to the west. She fled inside the *chaha'ooh*, but the thing locked a beam on it and nearly blinded her. When it finally moved on, the woman hightailed it over to my mother's place. My mother said she had come to realize that it was harmless, but she had been alarmed too at first. I asked my grandfather about it later. He didn't know what it was either, but he didn't seem too concerned. "There are things we don't know," was all he said.

Naanish

(Work)

I worked for the Navajo Nation government for several years, for the department of Food and Nutrition Services within the Division of Health. During that time I worked as a planner, information officer, adminstrative assistant, and administrative services officer. My favorite job was the position as information officer with the New Dawn program. The job involved daily interaction with my people and entailed extensive travel throughout my homeland. As the info person, I was responsible for the development and dissemination of information and educational materials in both *Diné bizaad* and English. I produced a newsletter, pamphlets, manuals, and videotapes explaining general and intensive gardening practices, as well other aspects of what is termed "appropriate technology."

139

The program was an ambitious attempt by a group of young *Diné* to do something about the chronic problems on the reservation related to food and nutrition. The pervasive poverty, generally low levels of formal education, high unemployment, ineffectual policies, and "benign neglect" by federal and state agencies, as well as decades of discrimination and prejudice, had created a situation where *Diné* health was suffering. Hypertension, heart disease, diabetes, and other conditions related to nutrition were prevalent in part because the people had experienced a drastic change in their diet and lifestyle. Over the past hundred years or so—just three or four generations, almost overnight in terms of human history—they had replaced a nutritious, high-fiber traditional diet based on corn, game, and wild plants with a contemporary diet consisting mostly of processed foods containing high levels of salt, sugar, fat, and chemicals. The people had also become more sedentary because they no longer had to raise, hunt, or gather their own food. Food could readily be obtained from stores. This pattern is endemic to many "developing" countries whose indigenous foods are supplanted by imports from industrialized countries. The result was a host of debilitating health problems that affected all segments of the population, particularly the young and the elderly. Several cases of kwashiorkor, a form of malnutrition commonly associated with "Third World" countries, were documented by the Indian Health Service on the reservation.

Additionally, most *Diné* were no longer self-sufficient. In contrast to the pre–Fort Sumner era, when *Diné* were completely self-sufficient and wealthy people, contemporary *Diné* are among the poorest people in the country. The per capita income in 1980 was $2,400. Public assistance and food-help programs provide sustenance for many families, but dependency has a devastating impact on self-esteem. In turn, low self-esteem contributes to a broad range of other problems. Alcoholism, suicide, domestic violence, birth defects, and a high mortality rate are some of the consequences.

A few families in areas that have enough water are able to maintain gardens, which supplement their diets. However, in most parts of the reservation there is no fresh produce available for much of the year. When it is available, the produce is often expensive and of inferior quality because it has to be shipped over long distances. Given the low incomes, most people simply cannot afford to buy them. The widespread use of chemicals in commercial agriculture is another consideration. Lastly, the ancient knowledge associated with traditional agricultural practices is also in danger of being lost.

The aim of the New Dawn program was to address these problems through the use of small-scale food production projects. We wanted to teach families how to grow their own food again, on their own lands, using what resources were available, so they could eat better and feel good about themselves. We investigated and demonstrated various methods of food production and preservation. We also promoted passive solar technology, especially in the use of greenhouses and home energy applications. Our most rewarding work, however, was the development of community seed banks, which were intended to perpetuate traditional crops. Such crops are ideal because they are acclimated to local conditions and the people already know how to grow them. We were able to rescue many native varieties of corn and squash. There is no feeling like seeing heirloom seeds sprout, and watching them grow and ripen, to give you hope.

Unfortunately, we were funded with federal money, and that meant we had to deal with Washington in addition to a whole slew of local bureaucrats and politicians. Sadly, our annual budget gradually shrank, while our requests for assistance from federal, state, and tribal sources went unanswered. We got a lot of promises and everyone agreed that self-sufficiency was important to *Diné*, but after five years of valiant effort the founders of the program, including myself, left in disillusionment. We were trying to do something, but we were only twenty-five people covering a 25,000 square-mile territory with over 225,000 people. Not until much later did we realize that in our youthful optimism we had failed to fully appreciate the scale of the thing we were facing. The situation we so desperately wanted to change is part of a global pattern that denies self-sufficiency to indigenous people in the interest of the industrial world.

Nelda and I leave at five o'clock in the morning to make it to a workshop at Crystal by eight. We are going to demonstrate transplanting techniques. A plywood cold frame holds seedlings in the back of the truck. Old Beige, the program's vehicle, is in a good mood this morning. After getting coffee and doughnuts at the 7-Eleven, we head down the shortcut toward the distant village snuggled against the western base of the Chuska summit.

Before long, we have entered the forest. "They say a lot of strange things have happened around there," Nel says.

"Uh-huh." I nod. "So I've heard."

"Believe that stuff?"

"Never seen it. Till I do—"

"Don't. It comes true if you say that."

"Hope not. I'm a big chicken."

"Well, we're passing through there soon."

A half-hour later we are on a stretch of road looping between thick stands of piñon. The trees are hemmed in by red cliffs to the east and west. Our headlights scare up rabbits and flying things. Nel fiddles with the radio as it fades in and out. Then we lose the last station. The cliffs block our reception. The heater whooshes. A dark horse standing beside the road jerks up its head and blurs past. *Yíiya!* I say to Nel. She giggles and pours more coffee from the thermos.

"Happened right about here," she says, peering into the shadows rushing past. "That story Ed told me about his in-laws from Farmington who got lost looking for a medicine man. I guess they had stopped at a house to ask for directions, but nobody was home. As they were pulling away, a big black dog ran out from behind the house and began following them. The driver speeded up, hoping to outrun it, but it kept chasing them. Later he stopped to send it back, but when he got out, it wasn't there. He thought it had gone home, so they drove on. A while later, though, he saw the dog behind them again. This time he slammed on the brakes so fast the dog almost ran into them. And here's the scary part: *It stood up*, to avoid running into the tailgate!"

"You're making this up, Nel."

"Listen, when that thing stood up, the driver lost it. He froze until his wife screamed, then he stomped on the gas. They did ninety down the road trying to outrun it, but it kept up easily with them. It even passed by them, somehow, and all of a sudden it was running in front.

"The wife was yelling and carrying on, and the driver said he couldn't think. He just did ninety, swiping bushes and stuff along the side of the road. Luckily, they saw another car coming and blinked their headlights. It slowed down and stopped. They explained what had happened, but when they looked around the thing was gone."

"Remember Janice telling about seeing one run straight up the side of a cliff? And didn't Robert once say that they can fly?"

Frank told this one: "One night this young woman was driving to Crownpoint from Kayenta real late, way after midnight. She was going over Narbona Pass. She knew that place had a reputation, but she wanted to get home. To save time, she had decided to drive straight through instead of staying overnight with friends in Tsaile. Near the campground just below the summit she suddenly felt the urge to pee, and since there were no cars on the road, she stopped. When she had finished, she noticed a pair of headlights approaching. She quickly got back in her car and locked the doors. She waited for the car to pass so she could pull back onto the highway, but the car stopped behind her and rolled up close. She got scared and put her car in gear and began to pull back onto the road. That's when the car behind her suddenly lowered its headlights, causing her to glance up into the rearview mirror. What she saw nearly made her faint. The driver in the car behind her looked like a bear! She saw the pointy ears clearly. She went blank with terror, but just for a moment. Then she snapped. She spun her tires and fishtailed back onto the road. The car followed right behind her, almost touching her rear bumper. In no time she was over the summit. Then they started down the east side, where the road drops four thousand feet in twelve miles. At the first curve, she noticed the car was trying to pull up alongside. She realized it could force her off the road if she let it, so she floored the gas pedal and a race began. Her old car roared, and the speedometer climbed to over ninety, but the other car kept up. Stopping was out of the question. She knew that the driver of the other car meant to kill her. She knew that even to look at the other car would mean certain death, so she kept her eyes glued to the road. She made it to the trading post at the foot of the mountains, but it was closed, so she pulled back onto the highway and headed south. Over the next twenty miles the two cars reached speeds in excess of one hundred miles per hour, and a couple of times she almost lost control. Several times she nearly lost consciousness, but she began praying, and that kept her awake and alert. She finally reached the all-night gas station at Tohatchi. She pulled into the parking lot and noticed that the car was no longer behind her. She stayed there until daybreak and then went directly to a friend's house. This friend was a medicine man

144

and she told him what had happened. He told her that she had been meant to die that night, but she had survived because she fought back. The skinwalker had been hired by the people her family had been having a land dispute with for years. She had been targeted because she had been the one writing letters and doing research to back up her family's case. Her friend conducted a ceremony for protection and she was able to go home."

In 1985 I leave the tribal government and work briefly for the Navajo Field Office of the Save the Children Federation. That summer, we gather fifteen hundred Native children from throughout the U.S., the Carribean, and Central and South America at Arizona State University near Phoenix. For four days we mingle, make friends, and learn about each other. We attend workshops, listen to inspirational speakers, sample traditional foods, and share dances and customs. On the final night, we gather in a huge banquet hall. Rows of china and crystal glitter before us. Bow-tied waiters bustle up and down between lines of dark-haired heads. Miss Indian America, a Hopi woman, entertains us with songs and a humorous talk about her experiences. The President of SCF exhorts us to reach for the stars. A "Just Say No to Drugs" message from Nancy Reagan is read. Billy Mills shows the famous film clip of his win at the 1964 Tokyo Olympics: The spectators cheer and rise to their feet as the runners enter the final turn, and with a burst of unbelievable speed he moves from a position at the rear of the pack, past a dozen or so others runners, and lunges through the tape at the last moment to win the gold medal. The crowd roars. There are tears streaming down the faces of people near me. It doesn't matter that the event happened many years ago, before most of the children present had been born, or that no Indian has won a gold medal since. What matters is that Billy

Mills is Indian, and so are we, and he won. Gradually the excitement subsides and Billy goes on to talk about his life.

Later, a group of Indian children from Guatemala step onto the podium. They are small and solemn. They are no older than most of the children in the audience. One girl has bright ribbons plaited in her hair. The boys, in their embroidered shirts and barbered hair, look straight ahead. With small quiet voices they tell us, through an interpreter, about what is happening in their homeland. Their families have been killed. The clatter of silverware dies quickly as their words sink in. The recognition, the pain and fear, is reflected in every dark face in the room. The radish on my plate, carved into a frilly rose, mocks me.

Earlier that day, at the Salt River Indian community center just outside Scottsdale, we had danced the Round Dance, drummed, sung our songs and shared a traditional Pima feast. I had marveled: the Children of the Condor, and the Children of the Eagle, at play! Just four miles away to the south, Sky Harbor International Airport, Arizona's gateway to the world, rumbled with air traffic. The towers of midtown Phoenix rose like broken teeth on the horizon. *There are jetliners circling overhead and those kids from Brazil are tasting their first ice creams and we are dancing,* I had thought. *We are still here!* But within the space of ten minutes those children had reminded us that so, too, are those who would massacre us.

Yootóódi ólta'

(The school at Bead Springs)

In 1988 I left the reservation again. I had been accepted into the creative writing program at the Institute of American Indian Arts in Santa Fe. It is a renowned art school for Native students, the only one of its kind in the country. Native (and non-Native) students from all over, including Alaska and Hawaii (and from throughout the world), come to learn traditional and contemporary arts. The school has produced some of the most accomplished Native artists working today. IAIA also has a lively creative writing program, which has graduated many of the better-known and up-and-coming Native writers.

As an art school it is unique enough, but as a *native* arts school IAIA has a special aura that is felt by everyone, student and faculty alike. We all know the critical importance of our

147

roles in perpetuating the voices, dreams, aspirations, and creative spirit of our ancestors and our peoples. That understanding of our sacred purpose and work there translated into a sense of what I can only term "spirituality," a feeling I have not had at any other school.

There were raucous times too, IAIA being a college after all, and even more because we were an *Indian* school (if you know 'skins, you know what I mean). Our unapologetic, natural and nonstop "differentness" flustered the *bilagáanaa* and *naakaai* students whose campus we shared. We didn't have to do outrageous things to be noticed, like pierce our eyebrows or dress in fancy clothes. In a small way, the balance of "privilege" was thus reversed, even if only temporarily, but in a way that nevertheless deeply and truly mattered.

The IAIA student body reflected the richness and diversity of the Native world: assimilateds and traditionals, urban and rural, full-bloods and cross-bloods, rich and poor, young and old. Within this mix, there were characters galore. Everyone had a story. Yellow Bird, a flashy Lakota transvestite, is especially memorable because IAIA shared the campus of the College of Santa Fe, a private Catholic school, and the majority of their faculty were nuns and priests. They raised their eyebrows but said nothing. What could they have said? We were a colorful bunch.

One day, during one of our usual Friday afternoon visits to art openings downtown, we were sipping wine on the balcony of a gallery above the courtyard on Water Street, talking about art, listening to piped classical music, and generally being rather sophisticated, when a group of European tourists standing by the railing began to talk animatedly among themselves and gesture at something below. Naturally, our curiosity was piqued, and we went over to see what was so interesting. It was Yellow Bird, done up in black lace like a señorita, clicking across the courtyard on high heels. It was an extraordinary moment. A startled elderly *bilagáanaa* couple scurried out of the way as, scarves fluttering and earrings flashing, Yellow Bird ascended the stairway to the gallery. The woman serving wine near the entrance was taken off guard only momentarily, then with a flourish she presented Yellow Bird with a glass of chablis. The tourists tried not to stare, but how could they not? They were intrigued by how blasé we Indians were about the whole matter. They loved it. This was definitely not something mentioned in their guidebooks.

Formerly, IAIA had occupied a lush campus directly across the street from the current location, but in 1985 the Council of the Eight Northern Pueblos appropriated it when the BIA boarding school in Albuquerque was closed and their children had nowhere to go. The College of Santa Fe graciously offered to lease a part of their campus to IAIA while funding was sought for a new campus. Some classes were shared with CSF and others were held in old army barracks. Not long ago, a local *bilagáanaa* corporation donated (returned?) a large parcel of land just south of the city for a new campus.

Henrietta, a Passamaquoddy from Maine, is stuck in my window. She and I have been partying for the past two weeks—actually longer, a whole semester, but who's counting? Anyway, this night I bailed out early and came on home, exhausted by the binge. Chicken, she called me, and turned around at the bar to talk to the black guy she'd been flirting with. I left and walked home, past the house where the Chicanos sat under the trees by their house drinking beer. "Hey, you," one guy said as I cut across the empty corner lot next to their house, "Stay off my property. That's my property, man." I swallowed my comment about it actually being stolen Pueblo land and walked on. I wanted nothing more than to get home, to get into bed and sleep. But now there's Henry, stuck in my window.

Get me outta here, she says, this friggin' hurts! I turn on the living room lamp and look away to keep from laughing out loud. I am pissed at her for bugging me in the middle of the night, but I can't help it. I laugh. There she is, big ass and all, wedged like a shoe in my window. I laugh again. Fuck you, she says. Get me outta here!

How did you get up there, I ask. Never mind, she says, just get me down. I push a chair under her dangling foot. Okay, now lean on me and slowly shift your weight onto the chair. Okay, you ready? Now! We struggle for a moment, me pulling and her straining against the tight squeeze. She keeps up a barrage of choice language, and finally, after a while, she spills into the room. She takes me down with her and we crash to the floor, breaking the coffee table in the process.

Hell, what were you doing? I ask. Don't you know what time it is? I fuckin' don't believe you! She starts crying right there. I'm sorry, she says, I'll just go. No, Henry, wait. Stay. Don't cry. But she cries, silently. I stand beside her, awkward, wanting her to stop. Finally, she stops and sits down on the couch. Where's that black guy you were talking to? Why didn't *he* help you? You're jealous! she says, almost triumphantly. I look at her. Jesus! She is even more amused. I knew it, you're jealous, she says.

In the morning I wake and push her heavy leg off me. Her hair is a mess. I go into the living room and look at the window. There are three narrow panes, two of which can be cranked open with a handle. One handle is broken off, and the pane is loose. I can imagine the landlord's reaction: "What *happened*?" How would I explain? I go outside and around to the side. That's how she did it. She'd dragged the neighbor's sawhorse to the window. I pick up the paper bag beside the sawhorse and stick the warm six-pack in the refrigerator. I hear her throwing up in the bathroom.

A couple months later, both Henry and I have left Santa Fe. I leave for California and she returns to Maine. Louisa, the sister-in-law she'd been babysitting for, has also graduated and returned to Maine. It is Louisa who tells me about the miscarriage.

Tóniteel bíighadi ólta'

(The school by the ocean)

From my window, Monterey Bay and the Pacific Ocean dominate the view. The city of Santa Cruz is spread below, the crescent-shaped sweep of buildings hugging the shoreline and spilling up the slopes of the surrounding hills, gleaming like a constellation against the dark mantle of vegetation. It is beautiful. The bay is dotted with whitecaps. The ocean sheens. From the broad meadow below my apartment where students gather daily to toss Frisbees or play tag football, the grassy hillside slopes down to the beaches and cliffs where waves crash endlessly. There, sea lions and otters loll on the algae-slick surfaces, squinting like whiskered old men in the spray of cold water.

On the municipal pier, tourists crowd elbow to elbow along the railings. They snap photos of each other posing beside the

153

gulls and huge pelicans that alight on the railing, while below sandpipers chase back and forth after the rolling waves, and fat shiny seals bob between the barnacle-studded pilings obnoxiously demanding handouts of fish from above. The fine *tourista mamasotas* are eyed appreciatively by groups of Mexican men who keep up a running commentary. An old Asian man fishes daily from the end of the pier, pulling out delicacies, eels and puffers, lionfish and stingrays.

The San Lorenzo River bisects the town—originally the site of an Ohlone village that was annihilated by the Spanish in the early 1700s—and flows languidly into the bay next to the Boardwalk, a large amusement park that attracts visitors from all over. Sometimes a huge school of anchovies will appear and turn the water around the wharf into a shimmering liquid silver. There had been annual salmon runs once, but after the redwood forests were cut down the river clogged with silt and the last big fish was seen long ago.

Santa Cruz is a resort town because of the temperate climate, picturesque cliffs and beaches, and the abundant marine life. It is also a haven for political correctness, burnt-out hippies, New Agers, surfers, college students, and a number of reclusive wealthy people. A major surfing competition is held in winter when monster waves born in storms off the coast of Japan reach the shore and roll through Steamer Alley thirty feet tall.

The town also hosts an odd assortment of outcasts and refugees who have established a community by the river. There is a sculpture of the Lakota leader Crazy Horse carved from white river rock and set on the north bank. It is the work of the Wildman, a burly redhead whose entire volcabulary consisted of a gruff "Arrgh!" The sculpture became a kind of shrine where people left offerings: feathers, stones, sprigs of greenery, flowers, candles, marijuana roaches.

Because of the climate and perhaps because of the supposedly progressive and liberal attitude in the town, Santa Cruz is a popular destination for drifters. In the late eighties they arrived daily, mostly young *bilagáanaa* men who haunted the bus station and adjacent pedestrian mall in the heart of the city. The drifters soon discovered, however, that they had not found paradise. The town, devastated by the 7.0 Loma Prieta quake of '89, used these drifters and the homeless as scapegoats. The citizenry vented frustrations on them. Local youths, proudly wearing red shirts as a symbol of their hatred, harassed them relentlessly. A strange war raged in the edenic setting for months, a fact pretty much ignored by the local press. But the stories leaked out anyway. The town instituted a curfew and banned camping, making outlaws of the homeless. For weeks, then months, the homeless protested by maintaining a vigil at the town clock tower. Eventually, though, even that was forbidden. The town fathers said that the protest allowed the homeless to violate the camping ban.

Strangely, while this was going on, the Save the Whale rhetoric continued unabated. Gay rights, multiculturalism, and a host of other worthy causes flourished. From my perch on the hill, I could descend into town and see all this. I went to the restaurants and bars, hung out in the swanky coffee shops and browsed the bookstores, but I had a place to return to. *Diné bikéyah*.

I looked on with interest and dread.

One day, Brian and Sharon and I are sitting on a hillside overlooking the ocean, talking and smoking. We are comparing our childhood experiences. After my story about Religion Day, as the Wednesday afternoon goings-on at my school back on the reservation were called, Brian said:

"Back in Modesto, we kids spent weekends and summers doing pretty much what we wanted. The only thing that spoiled that was when these missionaries came around trying to get us to come to their church. We were suspicious and hung back, but they offered bribes. Ham sandwiches, Kool-ade, potato chips. And if they really wanted us, ice cream.

"My folks worked in the fields, so we had to fend for ourselves most of the day. Compared to our usual beans and tortillas, that stuff was irresistible. We listened to their spiel for an hour or so, then they brought us home after we ate, in an old blue schoolbus with big white crosses painted on the sides.

"After a while we got tired of the routine though, even the ice cream. What they were making us do—sit still, pray and sing hymns—didn't make up for the loss of freedom. We began to dread Sundays. The neighborhood kids would shout a warning when they saw them coming: 'Run, kids! Here comes the Joy Bus!'"

We laugh and laugh. A couple passing by on the trail look at us curiously. They keep glancing back as they disappear into the woods. We sit in silence, lost in thought, watching the waves far below, until the meter maid's little vehicle appears at the bottom of the hill. Sharon sighs and gets to her feet, patting the dirt from her behind. Brian and I get up too, because those parking tickets are expensive. We walk slowly back down to the parking lot and drive off before the meter maid gets to the car.

Paige is an heir to millions, or so he said, but he lived in his battered orange van, a smelly dump on wheels. I met him one Saturday in the Blue Lagoon. I was to realize later that he was considered rather eccentric and held in disdain by some people. He was grungy, true, but that was only part of his persona. He was one of those people who are so brilliant they can't function in this world, or so it's said. He read Fredrik Pohl, composed music, was into video and avant-garde art, talked physics incessantly, wrote poetry, and made exquisite flutes. He was also a computer whiz as well as my ganja meister. We spent many days driving around, stoned out of our minds. We'd park by the ocean and watch the waves roll in. Some of the babes rollerblading by would wave. People knew him and they knew me because of him. "Hey, Tomás!" they'd yell when they saw me on the street. That was my made-up tag, my uncle's name actually, but the townies didn't know that. The city cops knew Paige well too. He'd been around so long, sleeping in his van, that he'd worn out his welcome. Because of the camping ban, he was forced to park in a different place each night. What kept him from being tossed in the slammer as a vagrant was his family's wealth. That meant influence. Still, he was harassed. He didn't seem to care. We often got his video equipment out of storage and taped hours of whatever caught our fancy. We edited those tapes into works of art and showed them to whomever we could lure into the van. People liked his productions so much they often asked him to cover special events. We taped parades, club gigs, parties, drag shows, weddings, and a couple of times some porn for people we knew, in a suite on the top floor of the Beach Comber Hotel, while tourists lolled on the sand below. The surprising thing about Paige was that he was a twin. Even more surprising was that his twin was his exact opposite, had a job, was "respectable," as his grandparents phrased it. His parents were movie star gorgeous and had a big house at Rio Del Mar. They seldom talked to Paige, though. The grandparents lived on the hill overlooking the Capitola wharf, an impressive address too. They didn't like him coming around too much either, he said, and constantly nagged him about his lifestyle. To be honest, I sometimes wondered about that too. He wasn't twenty-one anymore, but wasn't he still *bilagáanaa* and free?

When I met him, he had been out of work for nearly two years. His last job had been in the Silicon Valley. I met him when he asked me for a quarter in the bar. Later, he applied for and got food stamps. Before that, he lived on leftovers from McDonald's. He was tall and thin, with black hair and hazel eyes, descended from "generic European peasantry," he said, with a generous dash of "swarthy Mediterranean." He was extremely intelligent, and despite his appearance, he had relatively little difficulty with women. He introduced me to the people who hung out by the river. And he was the one who showed me Elfland, a magical place in the redwood forest above campus. There, in the fantastically shaped and burned-out stumps of redwoods lost to logging a hundred years ago, partyers and lovers burned candles and smoked pot. In a dense fog, you could imagine it really was the home of magical creatures. Narrow trails wound through the redwoods and ferny glades, through vines and shrubbery, rhododendrons and live oak. He sold ganja to the pale, sad-eyed waifs who hung out there.

When I left after graduation he had just been granted SSI benefits after the first try. His grandparents paid for the shrink who certified that he was wacko and unfit for employment. We laughed about that. He was planning to buy some ganja with his first check and maybe look for a place. As far as I know, he is in his van on a parking lot somewhere, listening to the thrash bands from "The City," smoking ganja, nibbling falafel, whittling flutes from bamboo or cutting them from steel tubing, and watching those incredible Pacific sunsets.

The Pacific Garden Mall, once a trendy pedestrian mall that had been the town's showcase, resembled a war zone. More than half of the historic brick buildings surrounding it had crumbled in the quake. Rows of gaping holes where basements had been lined the streets like graves. Trees with broken limbs huddled in their midst. Thick patches of weeds proliferated inside the squares of cyclone fencing. Bad as it was, things only got worse: a sudden overnight freeze later devastated the surviving vegetation.

The bookstore is housed temporarily in a tent. There are other tents like it up and down the street—boutiques, natural food stores, cafés. I am there one day, penniless, bored, looking for excitement. I am standing by the card rack, reading captions, when she walks in. A woman with short hair. I pay no further attention until I hear the name of that blonde Beverly Hills writer, Making-Big-Bucks-For-Selling-New-Age-Hokum-To-Unsuspecting-People-Woman, who claims to have been apprenticed by a number of unnamed Indian shamanesses. My ears perk up, and before I can check myself, a snicker escapes my lips. Both the woman and the clerk glare at me. I am a tall, dark man. They whisper. Then the clerk says, loud enough for me to hear, "Don't worry. I can call the police if he bothers you." I know the routine: The Cavalry. Uprising. Pacification. So I play along. I look away. The short-haired woman makes her purchase and hurries away, the feel-good spiritual salvation manual clutched safely under her arm. She throws me a look at the door. I catch a brief glimpse of the outside—leaves, trees, shrubs, the blue sky—before the door closes.

One day, Gail and John, Indian friends of mine, call me up. There is a sweat lodge being held, would I like to go? I have nothing else to do, so I say, why not? They pick me up later and we drive to the site, a secluded spot several miles out of town. There are a lot of vehicles parked alongside the fence. VW bugs, fancy cars, station wagons, trucks, vans. We get out and look around. A streamer of smoke rises from behind some bushes in a nearby field. We are spotted. A man approaches. He is smiling, but his eyes betray him. "Hiya, folks, glad you could come." But I get the feeling that's not what he means. "This way." He turns and we gather up our paraphernalia. Gail hesitates. Sweats are usually single-sex affairs, but this is California. Still. Then curiosity overcomes her.

There are about thirty people, one Indian man and the rest all *bilagáanaa*, gathered around a smoking fire. There are feathers and beads everywhere. A tape deck plays Forty-Niner songs. A woman dressed in a killer buckskin dress moves to the music, but her movements are all wrong. She's got her arms crossed stiffly in front of her chest. She bounces straight up and down, rigid. Her movements are jerky. Gail shoots me a funny look. The scene feels like some sort of hallucination. Someone brings us a pipe, bloodstone, decorated with an eagle feather. I look at John, who is Lakota. This is not in my tradition, so I hesitate. The man offers me the pipe, smiling. Should I decline? I look to John. "Here," John says, and takes the pipe. Gail, who is Tolowa-Yurok, is struggling with the same dilemma. John offers the pipe to the directions, murmurs a benediction, and blows smoke. Then he hands the pipe back. I see a different look come into the man's eyes, though he is still smiling.

Suddenly a man blows an eagle bone whistle. The people gather in a circle and stand holding hands. The tape deck blares. They begin shuffling in a counterclockwise direction, then the other way. Then they stop. They start touching each other: faces, arms, the whole body. They start undressing. We—John, Gail, and I—look at each other. I see Gail is disgusted. "Don't even bother," she says, "Let's get outta here." The Indian man stands amid them, looking embarrassed.

Months later, we run across the Indian guy. "How was your orgy?" Gail asks him. He is tipsy. We are at the Catalyst. He frowns. Then he laughs. We all start laughing.

Greg is German-Italian. His father is a high-powered government official and an important man in state politics. Both men are conservatives, though Greg will vehemently deny that he is. Like myself, Greg came back to school after several years of knocking about in the world. He is a navy veteran. The USS Saratoga. He has many marvelous stories about ports of call. Prostitutes, street urchins, drugs, tattoos.

He is a born-again Christian. We fight all the time, about everything under the sun, but we talk nevertheless. He is well-to-do, though he consciously tries not to show it. He dresses down meticulously, drives a cheap import, and carries no cash.

We drove to Tijuana once and visited the cathouses. We drank ourselves sick on tequila and looked in vain for the donkey show. There were Indians on the streets selling trinkets, their children huddled in cardboard boxes beside them. I cringed at the recognition. *I know what you are going through.* They spoke to me in Spanish and I wished I could talk to them. They were soft-spoken, small and dark. We were looking at their rings when some leathernecks came up and began harrassing them. "Get a job," they told the vendors, who looked up at them with tired eyes. "Take a bath." Greg surprised me by lashing out. The leathernecks looked at us with disbelief: the bleeding heart Squid and the darkie. Then the pack mentality clicked in, and they— all young *bilagáanaa* boys—poised to attack. We were outnumbered about six to one. I thought we were finished, but some Mexican cops saw what was going on and stepped between us, threatening stints in the local jail if we didn't behave ourselves. They told us to move on. I kept looking back, but the jarheads were going the other way, laughing and slapping each other on the back.

There is probably not one single right angle in the Kresge College provost's house. It is snuggled up against the armpit of the college, amid live oaks and redwoods. The college itself is a crazy maze of sharp angles and white stucco. Drooping handmade paper banners festoon the railings of balconies. *Stop the War! Bomb Saddam! Give Peace a Chance.* Inside the house, we are sipping wine and watching our host make pasta and a salad for supper. More wine. The day before, the students of Kresge College had announced their secession from the assemblage of residential colleges making up the UC–Santa Cruz campus. In the magical realm of gnarled oak and misty redwoods, the Independent State of Kresge had been proudly proclaimed.

One guest has left the table on the pretext of needing to use the facilities, but he is wandering around the house instead, investigating the weird angles and odd positionings of rooms. Right now he is in the office aerie above the living room and is looking through the triangular windows. He sees that down on the ground below, the rhododendrons and other shrubs are dripping with moisture condensing from the drifting fog.

This is definitely a long, long ways from home, thinks the wandering guest, but he is not lost or alone here. No, his journey to this house had begun years before when he came across the host's novel in the public library in Gallup, New Mexico, and he was entranced by the voice of a bear. Now here he is, wandering around in a crooked house, buzzing on wine, listening to jazz and wild stories drifting up from below: A drunk in love with an armless statue that he keeps in his garage. A woman who talks with animals. Pinch beans and socioacupuncture.

The ex-hippie old guard at UC–Santa Cruz were alarmed. The Reagan-Bush-era kids were driving Beemers and Saabs onto campus and demanding fraternities and sororities. Worse, these youngsters had the audacity to suggest that the newest residential college at the university be named Reagan College. They pooh-poohed the traditions the founders of the school held sacred—even the pass/fail grading option. Liberalism was under attack by the spawn of liberals. UC–Santa Cruz had been founded in the early seventies and its philosophy reflected the radical thinking of the sixties. The founders were proud that their school would be more human than traditional institutions. But now the old guard was afraid it was turning into the very thing they had abhorred. Freshmen were sometimes incredulous when told about the reasoning behind the selection of the banana slug as mascot. The use of the gastropod was a symbolic thumbing of the nose at aggression, at images of "warriors" and "braves" and the like. The old guard was aghast when vociferous supporters of Desert Storm stomped all over the spineless slug and tossed its mashed remains on the middens holding the ashes of burned draft cards and bras. Then again, the average family income of the students there was the highest in the entire UC system—in excess of one hundred thousand dollars per annum.

Dook'o'oosliid

(The San Francisco Peaks)

Going east. Home. As the plane crossed high
over the Colorado River, I leaned close to the window. I strained
to see things on the horizon. Familiar landmarks. For a while
there was only the vast brown desert, but then high over the
Valley of the Sun and the green wagon wheel of Sun City, I
saw the familiar blue cones off in the distance. The peaks rose
high above the floating brown layers of pollution, above layers
of earth reposing in the sun: the tan desert floor; the buff
sandstone of the Mogollon Rim; the red rock of Sedona and
Oak Creek Canyon; and the black volcanic debris by Flagstaff.
In early June, patches of snow lingered on the peaks. I could
not look away from the land until I saw, far away, the dim
outline of *Naalyé silá.*

165

Time passes quickly when you're having fun. There is a temporary job with the Navajo Nation. Old friends. A whole summer of possibilities. Then it is gone. I have been accepted into the MFA program at Cornell and I leave the homeland again, in the fall. Where am I going?

Táá'

(Three)

Travels in the Glittering World

Ha'a'aah biyaadi ólta'

(The school to the east)

I am on the other side of the continent, surrounded by an endless forest and a sky so low I can reach up and touch the clouds. Most days the air is thick with humidity and the vistas are obscured by haze. Trees crowd close on all sides, blocking my vision, making me feel claustrophobic at times. There is a stone staircase winding up from town that I climb often just to see beyond the dense walls of foliage. I am a child of the southwest, of unbounded and sunny expanses of mountain and desert. Here, I feel sealed within a membrane.

But I am in a city, though it is small and quiet. The transition is tricky, but I am not alone. She is *bilagáanaa* and *bíla'ashdla'ii*. A five-fingered. A human being. On clear days, the view from her flat is breathtaking. The long hill on the

169

other side of the lake is a tapestry of fields and trees and houses. Though she is a dyed-in-the-wool midwest girl and I am a dusky southwesterner, we communicate. I joke with her, my corny Indian jokes, and though she doesn't always understand, she smiles. I told her my name was Rolling Rock, and that I had a pedigree, referring to my Certificate of Indian Blood.

At the end of the spring semester in 1992, a friend and I embarked on a cross-country journey. We were going to attend a memorial powwow for a friend who had passed away the year before. The event was to be held on the Rocky Boy reservation in northwest Montana, near the Canadian border. From there, we would swing south along the eastern foot of the Rockies to Santa Fe, then Phoenix and southern New Mexico, and eventually back to New York. The trip took over three weeks, and it is among the more profound experiences of my life. For once, I saw the land close up rather than from thousands of feet in the air. I got a closer look at the people, too.

In some ways the trip—a journey that took us deep into the heart of the country—was a metaphor, a friend of mine observed, as I was struggling to describe what the experience had revealed to me about this particular place in time, this blip on the cosmic screen called America. Several things became clear. It seemed that the further west we went, the more obviously "Indian" we became, and consequently the more blatant people's racism became. We attributed that to a theory that the further west one goes the more cowboy-and-Indian the population gets—literally, in the case of Montana—and the fresher the memory of olden pioneer days is, with the parallel raw attitudes and treatment that result from that mix. We were no longer novelties, innocuous as we had been back east, where Indians make up a minuscule percentage of the population and other "minority" and ethnic groups receive the lion's share of attention, good and bad.

Out west, it was just *bilagáanaa* and Indian. The Indians were still around, alive and kicking, unlike back east, where they had been "extinct" for centuries. In the west, Indians are real and in general not highly regarded. Our saving grace was the New York plates on our car, which exempted us because it was understood that we weren't local Indians, the drunks from the local reservation who hung around town making fools of themselves, the ugly ones who don't resemble the beautiful Indians in the latest movies. We were different, "civilized," exotic, nonthreatening. We were from Back East. The main thing was that we were just passing through. And we had credit cards. Cold cash.

Our journey began in Buffalo, the onetime frontier town. We drove along the southern shore of Lake Erie and passed through the haze and humidity of Pennsylvania and Ohio that first day, skimming through farmlands and towns, skirting the urban sprawls of Cleveland and Chicago. I had never seen the midwest. It seemed to be all farmland, flat, intensely green, and muggy. We moved for hours along the edges of endless fields hemmed with windbreaks. The thick haze made the sky feel incredibly close, and that bred a sense of ominousness; even the sun was subdued and indistinct.

We stayed in Madison, Wisconsin, the first night. Going into the city, I didn't see much besides wide boulevards and a white dome amid trees and water. In the morning, we breakfasted in Eau Claire, in a squeaky-clean diner that was filled mostly with truckers at that early hour. They eyed us and talked among themselves. The land was amazingly green. We passed through Minneapolis and Saint Paul at noon and by nightfall we were in Fargo, North Dakota.

We had crossed an invisible boundary somewhere and we were definitely now *Indians*. My instincts crackled. The ability to quickly size up people is a skill most Indians develop by necessity. You learn to read people by their facial expressions, their body language, and by the tenor of their words and voices.

In the old days—and even now in some places—this ability could make the difference between getting by or getting shot. I think you have to be Indian, or at least non-mainstream *bilagáanaa*, to understand the feeling.

At one rest area in North Dakota a burly teenager with a buzz cut and a scraggly mustache, shit-kickers and John Deere cap, crushed a beer can and flipped it into the trash while looking at me. His buddies sitting in a nearby pickup truck laughed. I saw the gun rack behind their heads and for some inexplicable reason I wanted to laugh, but I looked away instead. I had gotten out to get soda from a vending machine and I had nodded—a major faux pas. Maybe they thought you were making a pass, my friend joked, but I could not enjoy the joke. That look. Over the course of the next several days "that look" would appear with increasing frequency, a barometer of sorts. My friend and I began counting the incidents. In the end, we tallied over one hundred "slights," as we called them, by the time we rolled into Phoenix two weeks later.

We arrived at Havre, Montana, in the late afternoon. We had dinner at a Pizza Hut and I was thrilled to see honest-to-goodness 'skins lined up at the salad bar, modern warriors lancing cherry tomatoes, sprouts, and croutons for supper. The town is the backdrop for some of James Welch's novels, and I was amazed to be there. I imagined that some of the characters could be at that very moment sitting at a bar somewhere nearby. After getting directions at a gas station we headed toward the reservation, which turned out to be just ten miles away. The road climbed up out of the carpet of cottonwoods lining the river valley and wound lazily toward brown hills. The land seemed dreary. I was beginning to fear that this would be a typical reservation, a tiny square of land in the middle of nowhere, a leftover scrap from the Land Grab that no one else had wanted, until we rounded the first hill and my jaw dropped. We pulled over and my friend took a photo of me standing by the car, a white moon hanging just above my head, and the forested peaks of the Bear Paw Mountains rising darkly beyond.

The story of the Rocky Boy reservation is fascinating. The Chippewa-Cree, who live there now, took refuge in these mountains in the late 1800s, driven there by *bilagáanaa* settlers who had coveted and wrested away the rich bottomlands and plains where immense wheatfields now checkered the earth to the horizons and beyond. Ironically, the Chippewa-Cree managed to retain this vestige of their homeland with the help of a *bilagáanaa* ally. The story of how they had been forced to hide in the mountains, sheltered in nothing but canvas tents over the long and bitter winters, is heartbreaking. The intervening years, however, had transfigured that tragedy into a victory. They are now in possession of the most beautiful land in that part of the state. They have their own schools, including a tribal college, and are pretty much self-contained in other respects. What had been a refuge, a last hope, has become a triumph, a potent testament to the power of the human will to survive.

The mountains aren't impressive seen from afar, even if they are the first mountains encountered upon leaving the plains, but once you enter into them and the ridges surround you, reaching into the sky, their forested slopes and clear streams beautiful beyond words, you can't help but be awed. To my mountain-starved eyes, they were truly magic. And the people were gracious hosts from the moment we arrived. After eating again at Della's house, we drove a few miles away, where a room awaited us in the home of our departed friend's brother. The road looped between peaks rising to unexpected heights above thick forests of pine, spruce, and ghostly white aspens.

In the morning, I went out onto the balcony and stood there in the chill. It had snowed lightly during the night, and the land was transformed into a realm of glittering ice and white powder. A pair of ducks paddled and quacked in the pond below the house. Other than that, there was absolutely no sound. I drew deep breaths of the clean, cold air. I called my friend's name silently and whispered a brief prayer of thanksgiving for being there, for having the privilege of seeing the beauty.

The powwow started in the evening, after the elders held a ceremony to remember the departed one. Hundreds of people came, literally the entire reservation population. A buffet-style dinner was laid out on long tables and the people filed past the offerings, everything from vension, pemmican, smoked salmon, and jerky to lasagna, steak, quiche, strawberry shortcake, and ambrosia salad. But before we began eating, the food had to be blessed with a prayer. And unbeknownst to me, a container of fat would also be passed around and everyone was expected to partake of it. When the container was given to me, I naively dipped out a heaping spoonful of the white stuff, thinking it was some kind of gruel, maybe cornmeal mush, because it had that consistency, and stuck the entire load in my mouth. My host gave me an amused but sympathetic look as I diplomatically moved the fat around in my mouth, resisting the urge to gag or spit it out. She laughed, at last, and sighed. "I know," she said. "I know."

The Grand Entry began promptly at six, and I felt waves of electricity surge up my spine. Goose pimples rose again and again on my skin. The drums boomed in the small gym, and the sound and the power reverberated inside my chest. *They say that the drum is the voice and heartbeat of this continent.* Over the next four hours I floated in the incredible energy unleashed by the music and dancing. The experience made all the anguish of being Indian bearable and precious. I was happy. I knew I would never give up my heritage no matter what the penalty might be, regardless of the suffering that would be inflicted upon me for refusing to assimilate, for remembering, for being a living reminder of the things some people would sooner forget.

In the morning we went to the cemetery atop the hill behind the village. Our friend's grave was covered with a star quilt, and small offerings from many friends sat around it, pottery from New Mexico, Iroquois baskets, tobacco, and a bouquet of wildflowers. It had snowed again, and low clouds were swirled in wisps around the peaks. There was a sensation of being above the clouds. The sky was incredibly blue and the sun dazzled. We looked out over the valley and the houses below. An eagle soared in circles high overhead. That made us feel good. We stood around his grave for a long time, sharing memories. And we cried. He had been a rising star in Indian Country, a gifted scholar, a new force in the world and a hope for Indian people, but he'd died suddenly and now there we were, Indian people gathered from all over, New York, Oregon, Colorado, Arizona, Texas, Oklahoma, and California. I let my eyes drift slowly across the panorama, for I knew I might never see it again. I wanted to try to see this land he loved as he might have seen it.

We left the following day, and for the remainder of the trip all we talked about was the powwow and the beauty of the Rocky Boy reservation. A month later, I was back in the *bilgáanaa* world, but I had the memories. The voice of the drum was still inside me.

Halgaii hatééł

(The Great Plains)

Going home. Westward. That is so alien to me, that grid spread out like a checkerboard below, from horizon to horizon. But who would understand my anguish? I am filled with a rush of sorrow. *Nahasdzáán shimá*, what have they done to you? The whole story is laid out right there: the enormity of what has happened to us and to you, my mother, staggers me. I feel like weeping. My eyes seek something natural, a river, a bit of eroded ground, anything that isn't so damned symmetrical. The roar of jet engines fill my ears. The people laugh at something on the television monitors. I close my eyes. I can't take it. I flee into the restroom and rock in the turbulence.

I come back later dry-eyed and look down again. I know the story, the meaning behind this invention, this marvelous streamlined machine I am ensconced in, the plot of that movie,

177

the punch lines, the crescendoes, and I know the Myth. Discovery. Manifest Destiny. Civilization. Progress. The irony is not lost on me that the Breadbasket of the World below, dark and rich with our blood, feeds us too. Bleached commodity flour once a month. Commodity rice, commodity beans, commodity this and that.

We hang over the land for a long time. Invisible currents make the wings shudder. Ginger ale fizzes in my glass. Rivers branch and flash like lightning below. The man next to me is reading about investments. I am hurtling through the air, while below *Nahasdzáán shimá* lies bound and gagged.

Much later, I sit up. There they are, the mountains. I say the names in my mind. Pike's Peak, Spanish Peaks, and *Sisnaajiní*, the home of *tséghá'dínídínii ashkii* and *tséghá'dínídínii at'ééd*, Rock Crystal Boy and Rock Crystal Girl. I feel the power seeping back into my body.

Áhálą́anee'.

The Book of the Dead

The sky is clear for once and the sun shines. I walk toward the bus stop downtown. My neighbor, an elderly *bilagáanaa* woman, says hello. She is shy and generally avoids strangers. I smile and nod. A Tibetan monk in a maroon-and-gold robe, one of several living in the monastery down the street, is sweeping the sidewalk. He bows and smiles. A few minutes later, I'm at the bus stop.

"Mornin'," says the driver.

I make my way to the back and sit beside a *bilagáanaa* guy who gives me a quick little smile. The weather is making people agreeable. The winter harshness has had people on edge for months.

The bus labors uphill.

I get off at an intersection near campus. The air smells of damp earth. I stop for a moment on the stone bridge over the gorge and watch the stream frothing below. It makes a hushing sound as it fans over the rocks. The houses along the rim are outlined sharply, and here and there people have hung out laundry on porches and balconies. They make colorful blotches like flowers against the solid backdrop of trees and bushes.

As I walk up toward the student union, the bells of the clock tower begin to clang. Students hurry between classes. They part like water around me. Their voices fill the air. On the grassy slope above the campus store, couples hold hands and kiss.

I stand for a moment outside the gray stone student union, looking at the ivy, the bell tower, and the squirrels dodging bicyclists. Then I turn into the arching entryway and the ornate lobby.

There is a carnival atmosphere inside. Campus groups have set up tables in the lobby and students cluster around them. There is the smell of popcorn and someone plays the piano in the Memorial Room.

I go down the stairs, pausing now and then to let students rush past. A girl bumps my bag as she bounces past me. I hear a thock. She rubs her elbow and looks at me accusingly. I shrug and smile. It was not intentional. She turns back to her friends. They make the last turn and disappear through the gold doors of the dining hall. I follow them and pause just inside. The place is jammed.

There are hundreds of students. Their voices drone. There is the clink of silverware and plates. Music blares from the jukebox. I move over beside the condiment station.

The table nearest me is full of baseball caps, white turtlenecks, and flannel shirts. They are talking and don't see me. I smile at no one in particular and look around. The next table has more of the same. I look closely in case there is someone I know. I don't see anyone, so I swing my bag around. The first slug shatters a glass of milk. There is a millisecond of stunned silence, then they begin to scream and run.

I am inside this dingy place right off the Commons. It's lowlife, but where else can I go? Not those pretentious preppie hangouts. Not those jock places. *The looks they give you.* Anyway, here I am, hanging on for dear life to a bottle of Rolling Rock. I've had several already. I don't care what anyone thinks of this. I see what I see, feel what I feel.

Brother Elias told me, back at Santa Cruz, that he *understood*. I agreed with him then because I needed an ally. And he was. But my anguish is my own. Brother Elias has his pain too.

The bartender lingers down at the other end of the bar. I signal him and he brings me another. "Thanks," I tell him. *Thank you for your mercy. This anesthesia.* I light another cigarette and blow smoke. I wish it was that easy. Lighter than air. An easy way to live. But no. I am here. I am brown. I know I am too far from home.

What are they saying? That old woman and her man. They're looking at me. The look is not friendly. At least they're honest. Fuck P.C. Call a wagonburner a wagonburner. Don't be afraid. Don't mince words. I've heard it all before. In the end we know who bleeds. Whose life.

The woman says something to the bartender and they all look at me. I return the favor. The entire history of this continent stretches between us like concertina wire. My Indians lean back on their horses atop the ridge. Their settlers draw the wagons into a circle. The woman scowls. That's right. There's this myth about pioneer *bilagáanaa* women, that they stayed home, gardened and mothered, milked the cow and pretty much served as the repository and champion of Civilization in the wilderness. But there she is, alongside her man, hunkered down behind the barricade, sighting down the barrel, centering the crosshairs on my dark face. It's all been decided. The Indians will ride away and the settlers will go on victorious. I look at myself in the mirror behind the bar. I wish I was not so Indian-looking. Maybe then I'd have some peace.

Why don't you go somewhere else? my friend has said. Where? Mars? The moon? This is my home, goddamn it! The woman laughs loudly and takes a deep drag of her cigarette. I look at her in the mirror. She exhales smoke from her nose. Her companion doesn't look at me. She says something and he snickers at her remark. The bartender is a wimp. He laughs, but he looks embarrassed. He doesn't look at me. He knows I'm watching. He feels my Indians flexing their fingers, itching for his scalp. "Ah, jeez," the woman says loudly and stares at me. The contagion spreads. The old men go silent. Oh, I know they'll pass maximum sentence. The rock pile. Bread and water. Solitary. But this is just speculation? Heck, no. If anyone's making a big deal, it's them. What could, or would, I do? Spread a disease? Bring down God and country? I just want my beer. *That place? You know damn well what'll happen there!* I do. Same thing that'll happen at the fancy place down the street. Same thing as the jock place. The snooty coffee joint. At least here they're uncomplicated. No fancy rationalization. No affirmative action or multiculturalism here.

I talked to Clarisse yesterday. She suggested a story for the paper, but I don't want to get into sports mascots. What about those damned posters and stuff all over town? Especially the one advertising pills and potions in the window of that health food store, that *bilagáanaa* guy on horseback, in dyed turkey feathers, cheesy suede vest, and Hong Kong beads, the caption proclaiming: *They knew the power.* My ass! If they—meaning Native people—knew the power, why didn't they survive? Where are they? Hiding behind the kitschy shield that's a nameplate for that exotic goods store in Center Ithaca? In that children's book at the Pyramid Mall? *One little, two little, three little Indians . . .* "Isn't it wonderful?" the clerk had gushed.

182

"It's selling so well." No doubt. No wonder things are so screwed up. Why don't they tell the truth? Isn't truthfulness supposed to be a Christian value?

That woman sure has a problem. I think I'd better go. I'm not running from them, mind you. I'm running for my life. My Indians want to get off this goddamned hill. They know they're no match for the Howitzers, the Hotchkiss and Gatling guns. Well, lady, you win. This place is yours. This bit of America is safe again. And we *do* know our place. It's been drilled into us from birth—how can we forget? The bartender says, "Do you want any more?" Fuck, no.

It's raining lightly. I am on my way to the bus stop. There is something going on when I turn the corner onto the Commons. A crowd is gathered in front of the center stage. I recognize the Tibetan monks who live down the street from me. They are lined up on the stage with several of their countrymen. There are placards behind them condemning the Chinese invasion and occupation of Tibet. The signs tell of genocide and oppression. A *bilagáanaa* man, identifying himself as a sponsor, talks about what has happened to these people. I listen to the story and I want to go up to those people—the monks and their young people standing up there with them—and touch their hands. I know how they feel, what they're talking about. People stand around, a field of trenchcoats, handmade wool sweaters, red-and-white umbrellas, earnest faces. There are a number of reporters and an on-the-spot television crew. They are eating this up. After the man finishes, the Tibetans sing their national anthem, a haunting melody. I feel tears threaten then, and I take a deep breath. There is a moment of silence after the last notes of the song. Then the people push forward to speak to the Tibetans and sign their petitions on a table beside the stage. I go up and shake hands with a young Tibetan man. I am a native of this continent, I tell him, and I know what you're talking about. He looks surprised, then he bows and smiles. People press in, chattering.

I turn and begin to walk away. A reporter scurries after me. He wants me to comment on the event. I know why he's asking me. It has to do with validation. My brown stamp of approval. I stop and pretend to ponder a response. His pen hovers eagerly over his clipboard. "Well," I say, "the irony certainly is not lost on me that these Tibetans are asking for support from a people who are guilty of genocide and oppression too, as well as the illegal occupation of this hemisphere." He is stunned for a moment, then he simply looks disgusted. He turns away and I hurry on to catch my bus.

I want to kill, but I know I won't. I can't. It's impossible, legally and morally. Instead, I will turn the gun on myself first.

We are driving around west Buffalo when Jack notices we're low on gas. We pull over to a gas station and Jack goes in to pay first. There is a black couple standing at the counter, talking to the clerk. I see them through the window. They glance at Jack, at someone standing out of sight beside him, and then back at each other. Jack leans around them and hands the clerk his money. He comes back out and begins pumping the gas. I roll down my window to let in some air. The couple emerges and get in their car. A young blond *bilagáanaa* woman comes out after them and walks over to a family who pulls up in a Jeep Cherokee. She goes to the driver's side and stands there talking for a few moments. The driver, a man, keeps shaking his head. Finally the woman turns toward us. It is chilly, but she is wearing only a sweater and jeans.

"Hey," she says, "can you guys give me a ride?"

"We're getting on the Skyway," says Jack.

"Please, I'll pay."

"Really, I'm sorry."

"I've got three dollars." She starts digging in her pocket.

"We can't." Jack stares at the pump.

"It's just up the road." She points.

"Sorry."

I remember that my window is open. Jack's voice is unmistakable. There's something about her. She could just reach in. She keeps talking. Jack finishes and gets in. As we are pulling away, the woman is walking toward another car in the parking lot.

"Whew," says Jack. "When I was inside, waiting behind that couple, that girl says to the black woman something about 'Don't fuck with me, I've got a knife.'

"The black woman doesn't realize the girl is talking to her at first, then she looks at her companion and says, 'Is she talking to *me*?' The black woman looked like she could handle the girl easily, but the girl says it again. No white girl in her right mind would say that to a black woman, Jack says. The black woman decides to let the remark pass. We realize there's something wrong with the girl, psycho, high on drugs, something."

Later, a car begins following us, honking. Shit, says Jack. The car follows for a couple of blocks. We ignore it, but it speeds up and pulls up beside us at a traffic light. The driver and the passengers, *bilagáanaa boys*, yell something at us. We look straight ahead. Later, another car drives by and the driver honks. I sneak a look and the driver points at something on our car. "He's pointing at your car," I say. Jack pulls over, joking about muggings because we are in a deserted unlit area. Jack gets back in. "The gas cap was off," he says. "It was sitting on top of the trunk." We laugh. A few minutes later, he says, "And I want to go to *New York*?" Jack has just interviewed for a job.

Terra Incognita

I delay as long as I can, then I really have to go. Jack has told me to meet him for lunch before I return to Ithaca. Manhattan is twenty minutes away. Not far, but I am nervous. Maybe I shouldn't have done that number. Oh, well. The window above the sink is street level and I see dogs and knees go by. I'm at Jack's apartment in the Bronx. Finally I screw up the courage and gather up my stuff. It is drizzling and I am relieved because it has driven most people indoors. I walk slowly, nevertheless, drawing out the minutes. Then I am climbing up the stairs to the kiosk and the turnstiles, and my heart is in my throat.

I clutch the token and pace up and down the platform. There are only a dozen or so people. I settle on a bench to wait, but an old man sees this and attempts to strike up a conversation. I nod, but I wish he would go away. There is something about him. The train arrives at last and I get aboard as close to the middle as possible. Then we're off with a slight lurch.

The red brick buildings flick past and I focus on the distant outlines. I feel so conspicuous. Everyone must know. I steal looks at the people around me. A man reading the paper. A young girl holding the hand of an even younger girl. A couple twining limbs. An older woman whose face is an empty slate. Several guys in baggy clothes and headphones. Here I sit in my leather jacket, a sitting duck, a billboard advertising naïveté. I realize I'm clutching the bag I'm carrying a bit too tightly. Dead giveaway. Mug me, my shoes scream.

With every stop more people get on, and soon all the seats are taken. I smell perfume and something funky. My nerves are humming. A black girl directly across watches, big gold hoop earrings swinging with the motion of the train. Suddenly we are plunged into darkness. The interior lights are harsh and the girl isn't so young, I see. Her lips are bright red. She isn't watching me after all.

On the other side of the Harlem River a group of Germans board and stand swaying in front of me, cameras and purses carefully guarded. One has a skinhead look. They don't see me. Just an anywhere brown face. There is a vinyl jacket, a gorgeous blond woman, a couple of Arab guys. Black Leather Jacket enters at the next stop and towers over the Germans, though they're no shrimps either. I see my face in the lenses of his shades when I glance up. He scowls. Don't stare, I tell myself.

"First time?" says the girl beside me. She is holding a gym bag and looks at me closely.

"Yeah," I admit.

"Thought so."

"I'm going to Grand Central Station," I volunteer, but she has lost interest.

I grope in my bag and pull out the first thing I touch, our weekly tribal paper.

The sun bleeds color into the clouds. It rained last night and frogs croak away by the stock pond. Paul puts the last of my bags into the trunk and slams it shut. I am still inside, lingering over coffee. Mom says, "Write, okay?" "I will," I promise. "You never do," she corrects. "The writer in the family, and you don't," she says. Behind her the television on the counter flickers with images of urban violence. "Write," she repeats and places her hand on mine.

I kiss my niece and nephew, Kimberly and Edwin. My babies. Then it's off down the road. I glance back one last time before we round the bend behind the village and pull onto the highway. Even then, I scan the forested slopes of the mountains. What is it about you and mountains? a Seneca friend in New York had asked. I think about this as we drive. *Naalyé silá.* In the morning light the summit is cast gold.

"You're a masochist," says Paul, my brother. "I don't understand what you see out there."

I don't answer. My life. By midnight I am back "there." In the city. The sirens welcome me. Lights wink and shine. The cabbie takes the tip without a word. I collect my mail and climb the squeaky stairs to my apartment. The tribal newspaper has come. I fix some coffee and settle on the couch with the paper I've read already at home. The news seems fresh. A whole world out there. *La tierra de pico tiempo.*

Peace and quiet.

A bump and a grunt startle me. He is trying to fit his big butt into the small space beside me. He mutters as he waggles his ass. I hitch my rear sideways, but there is no room. He comes down, muttering louder. I smell underarms and fried chicken. He is huge, jelly gut hanging down. He is breathing loudly, rasping, and pulls something from the pocket of his coat. He starts to eat right there, tearing chicken skin with his teeth. A big drop of grease runs down his hairy wrist into his sleeve.

R. stands there, watching me watch Arnold demolish a high-tech set on TV. "Why?" he says. The motel room is steamy from the shower. The towel around his waist is barely hanging on. A dark wispy line curls from his brown belly into the towel. Water drips from his hair onto his shoulders and chest. Thirty year-old love handles. I reach over and smear one drop. He stops me. "Stick to the question."

"I don't know."

"That's really pathetic."

I am speechless. Arnold. Jet engines. Car exhaust. The smell of Chinese food. He dresses quickly as I sit there in my sunburn and day-glo red trunks. He says, "I have to go."

"I have to go, too," I say.

"Protest March!" says the headline. The three *bilagáanaa* teenagers who'd killed a *Diné* man in Farmington, one the son of a judge, had been sentenced to two-year terms in reform school. "Slaps on the wrist," said Fred Small Canyon, an organizer of the march. "They did the same thing twenty years ago. This wouldn't happen if the victim had been white." He stands, fist raised and defiant, in front of a large crowd carrying placards. *We demand justice! We are human beings!* That same day another *Diné* man is killed in the parking lot of a grocery store, his skull crushed by a shopping cart launched like a missile by a *bilagáanaa* boy on a speeding motorbike. "I didn't mean to hurt him," claimed the sixteen-year-old boy. His parents were at a loss. "We're Christians, we don't hate nobody," said the mother. "We've lived here more than ten years We have lots of Navajo friends. My husband works with them." On page two there are six auto accidents reported, with nine fatalities. There are also three homicides, two rapes, and a suicide. On

190

page three the tribal council scorned its own laws and authorized the expenditure of fifteen million dollars for capital improvement projects, sucking up the last of the mandated fifty-five million dollar reserve fund. On page four charges of environmental racism were leveled at several corporations trying to establish toxic waste dumps and storage sites for nuclear waste on Indian lands. In the letters section a concerned citizen from Paducah complained that Indians were wrongly bad-mouthing New Agers. On the back page, Tony Hillerman expressed surprise at a press conference in Gallup when a *Diné* reporter questioned his use of *Diné* culture, especially in his hugely popular string of whodunits.

As we slow for the stop, Jelly Belly heaves himself up with a string of popping farts. I jump to my feet and press into the bodies that are edging away too. Moments later I am swept out the doors in a near stampede. I make my way past the guards, up the stairs, and across the colossal room. From the top of the stairs on the other side, I stand looking back down for a moment. Ants. Then I step out into the drizzle.

"Umbrella?" urges a black vendor.

"No," I tell him.

"Why not?" says Jack, who is suddenly at my elbow. "Ready? I know this place down the street."

It's amazing how quickly I fall into pace.

Díí

(Four)

From the Glittering World

The Snake of Light

I.

Set on a bed of ash and embers, the pile of kindling smoldered thickly before igniting finally into tiny flames that grew quickly, building up steadily in power and resonance until the fire rose up the stovepipe with a hollow roar. Slowly it subsided, quieting in a while to a steady crackle that could barely be heard through the iron walls. Nearby, a kerosene lamp burned dimly atop a small, square table draped with a worn and faded oilcloth. A moth fluttered around the lamp, trying to reach the glowing flame inside, but it was repulsed again and again by the hot chimney glass. Scorched, it whirled away and careened erratically about the room. In time, it dropped onto the tabletop and whirred in ragged circles.

The room was small, octagonal, and the dim lamplight scarcely illuminated it, reflecting off the pine logs with a dull,

195

bronze-orange glow. Along one section of the wall, a narrow cot sagged under a tattered quilt, next to a stack of suitcases and cardboard boxes covered with a towel. An old flour sack served as a curtain for the sole window.

Outside, the wind pulled streamers of smoke away from the *hooghan* into the gathering darkness. Aside from the whir of moth wings and the subdued crackle of the fire, the room was empty of sound and motion.

Presently, however, there was a noise at the door. The doorknob turned and the door swung open. An elderly woman entered. She was laden with an armload of wood and her movements were slow. But it was more than just the weight of wood that slowed her. She was old, and there were things on her mind. She dropped the wood into the box by the door and rubbed her back. This kind of thing was getting to be too much for her. *But who would do these things for me?* she wondered.

She sighed deeply and glanced across the room at an object that was propped amid the clutter of things on the towel covering the suitcases and boxes: a hand-tinted photograph set in a silver frame. It was the portrait of a young man in military uniform.

In the eyes of the old woman, the picture moved; the dark eyes shone and a shy smile creased the corners of his mouth ever so slightly. But that was impossible. It was an illusion, and she knew it. He was gone, vanished from her world as if he had never existed at all. *"Shee'awéé,"* she murmured. She had never stopped thinking of him as her baby.

The night was one rendering of reality, and the thoughts preoccupying the old woman, another. In a span of years, her dwelling upon memories had become a salve for the deep ache of his absence and the stark silence she lived with day after day. Now and then she stirred from her thoughts to lay more wood on the fire, or to sip coffee from a blue enamelware cup.

In time, a second moth emerged from the shadows and flew circles around the lamp. But she did not see it. The moth itself was insignificant, a shadow, but the incessant whir of its wings sparked the memory of a voice in her mind. Without thinking, she mouthed a single, silent word: *Ashkii*. The word was a name, and the name is a portal into her thoughts. Her mind had left the room and slipped seamlessly into another world.

She was a younger woman suddenly. *"Ashkii!"* she called from under the arbor. He was playing on the bank of a small wash nearby and pretended not to hear. She knew though, that he'd heard and would come soon enough. His stomach will remind him of the stew that's simmering on the fire and the frybread I'm making, she thought, and laughed softly to herself. He would wolf it down and ask for more.

They were alone, the woman and boy. Both her man and her only child, a daughter, had gone on years before. The boy was her grandson and sole heir. At times his mere existence was such a medicine to her that she would wonder what it might have been like without him. But his presence was also a constant reminder of the circumstances of her daughter's death. It hardly seemed possible, sometimes, that ten years had passed since that cold spring morning when he was born and her daughter had died. He didn't know that she had pulled him from her daughter's body when it finally ceased to struggle, and that she had been afraid he was dead, too, until he screamed. After that, she had been fiercely determined that he should live.

Sometimes, when he struck a certain pose, or said things in a certain way, the resemblance was so unnerving that her throat would tighten. But then, he had other features too, and inevitably she would think bitterly about the unknown swain who was his father. *"Ma'ii ni!"* she would mutter. She hated the coyote who had tricked her daughter.

The years slipped by quickly, so quickly that just the summer before she had been astounded to realize one day that he stood nearly as tall as she. Looking back, she saw that their lives had been like the land around them, the days melting into years like the hills and washes receded into oneness with the vast desert. She kept busy at her loom while he went out with the sheep each day, into the wide valley in search of pastures for the sheep and what adventures a young boy's imagination might create out of the hot sands and long hours of solitude. She made jerky and parched corn for him to take along and taught him to find water in the thick flesh of roots and cactuses.

One day, a strange cloud of dust appeared on the horizon at the far edge of the valley. Instinctively, the old woman sensed that something was going to happen. The dust looked to her like a whirlwind. Whirlwinds were forces that could disrupt a person's harmony with the land. Something that powerful had the power to lay life paths askew. She watched it descend into the valley and felt her scalp prickle. It was coming straight across the valley, toward her home.

It moved slowly, awkwardly, making its way laboriously around clumps of rabbitbrush and greasewood anchored in high dunes. In the hot, still air of the valley the dust rose sluggishly and hung suspended in the shimmer of heat waves. She saw that it was attached to the earth with a dark object; far off and small, it resembled a black ant, but as it came closer she saw that it was a truck. Her heart quailed. *Bilagáanaas! Bilagáanaas* were said to be taking children from their homes to keep in their schools. She told him to run quickly into the hills with the small sack of jerky she pressed into his hands, and stay there until they had gone back across the valley. He shot her a wide-eyed look and she felt a small wash of relief swirl within her, but then she saw his eyes fix on the approaching machine.

In that instant, the consequences of the truck's appearance struck her. She felt a balance shift, something in the turn of events that threw their world off kilter. She wanted, somehow, to show him that the truck was dangerous, but she didn't know how. Instead she could only motion to him urgently and watch him as he turned slowly and walked away.

It disturbed her that he was intrigued by the very thing she feared the most: the alien world of the *bilagáanaa*. Unwittingly, her hands clenched themselves into fists. A swell of emotion rose inexorably within her and threatened the thin cage of her chest. They had, in a way, captured him already. With that understanding, she watched the approaching truck with fear, then hate, in her eyes. She might have felt better if the dog had stayed to challenge the machine with her, but it had followed the boy and she had to face the coming encounter alone. She took her place under the arbor and watched the truck crawl across the valley.

After a long time, the truck rolled to a stop a short distance from her home. She did not stir. She stared at the men as they climbed down from the truck. They were sweating and the perspiration glistened on the bald head of the taller one. They approached her cautiously, as if sensing the hostility boiling within her, but they approached nevertheless and stood before her. She sat still, looking past them to the heat waves in the valley. She did not acknowledge their presence until the tall one cleared his throat. She looked up then and directed a cold stare into his blue eyes. He looked away. "Yá'át'ééh, he said, greeting her in her own language. She was not surprised and ignored his proffered hand.

"Aoó." She acknowledged their presence mechanically.

She did not invite them into the shade of the arbor, and they stood shifting from one foot to the other in the hot sun. They squinted in the brilliant light and the short one shaded his eyes with a soft, pink hand. Sitting in the deep shade of the arbor—like an animal poised defensively in its lair—she could see them better than they could see her.

While the tall one talked, the short one surveyed her home. His eyes narrowed at the sight of her old cribbed-log *hooghan*, the juniper post corral, and the makeshift arbor. The tall one's command of the language was poor, and his voice boomed offensively in her ear, but she understood anyway. They had come to take her grandson. It is the law, the tall one said. If the boy did not go with them now, they would have to notify the Bureau police. "You wouldn't want to get into trouble with *them*, would you?" he asked her, drawing himself up to his full height. "*Ndaga*'," she said. She wanted no trouble with anyone. She was an old woman, but had she been younger, it would have been different. She would have wrestled the both of them to the ground. They shot startled glances at each other.

She stared at them steadily, but they averted their eyes to the tangle of brush and boughs covering her arbor. *He is all I have*, she told them. *He is my arms and legs now that age is beginning to weigh upon my limbs*. They could understand that, couldn't they? Didn't they have children too? But they persisted.

The sun blazed relentlessly. Slowly it began to descend from its zenith and the heat intensified in the lowering angle. The land became fiercely hot. The *bilagáanaas'* shirts soaked through with sweat and they retreated into the scant shade cast by the hogan. From there, they continued their harangue. Finally, she got tired of them and got up. "*Dooda*," she told them, they could not have him. You simply did not take children from their homes. More than that, she could teach him all he things he needed to know. She shook the sand from her skirt and walked past them into the *hooghan* and closed the door.

They knocked several times, but she remained motionless inside. After a while, she heard the truck doors open and close. Then the engine roared to life. She listened to the truck moving away until it she couldn't hear it anymore. Then she opened the door and leaned against the doorjamb. She clasped her thin arms around the ache in her chest and felt tears well up in her eyes. She knew they would not give up so easily.

She stirred from her thoughts and got up; the fire had died down and the stove was silent. She poked at the few remaining embers with a bit of kindling and blew gently. Gradually, the wood succumbed and burst into flame. Satisfied, she returned

200

to her chair and sat down slowly. She put a piece of cold, rubbery tortilla in her mouth and chewed absently. Once more, her mind propelled her from the room into another reality.

It was spring. The sun was warm, well on its way back from the vernal equinox, and a fine patina of green smudged the contours of the land. Her eyes kept vigil on the far horizon: soon he would come. Images of her grandson swam in her mind. He is now twelve. They had kept him two winters already, returning him in the spring and reclaiming him in the fall. The brief months she had him with her provided her with a wealth of memories that sustained her when she was alone.

And hate sustained her. She hated them so much she clenched her teeth and looked to the hills to distract herself from the awful thing that was happening. "*Áhálaanee'*," she said, and felt a rush of love. She had wanted to take him and flee with him into the hills, but she understood the futility of that and had turned painfully away. They had vehicles and men.

Ironically, it had been Navajo men, not *bilagáanaas*, who came for him one day. "*Dooda . . . áshoodí . . . shiyáázh*," she had begged them, calling them grandson, son, but they'd turned a deaf ear. She had even tried to wrestle with one of them, but he'd broken free of her grip and stayed beyond her reach, making full use of his youth and agility. She had cursed and shouted, but to no avail. In the end, she had closed the door behind her and shut her eyes. She covered her ears to block out the sound of his screams as they dragged him away. After he was gone, she'd sat for a long time under the arbor, holding in her palm a bit of sand scooped up from his footprints.

The first time they brought him back, he jumped from the still-moving truck and ran to her, becoming suddenly shy at the last moment. But he hesitated only momentarily, then he was himself again, talking and gesturing so fast she had to laugh. He chattered about things he'd seen and done and strange words rattled off his tongue, but she only half-heard them. She touched his face with her eyes and listened to the changes. The strange words he used, and the new inflections on familiar words, were stark revelations of what they had already done to him. She realized with a sinking feeling that it would be like that from then on, that there might be no end to it.

As the years passed, she both feared and looked forward to his return from the *bilagáanaa's* school. She learned to anticipate, and ultimately accept, the changes he influenced in her world. It was only because he was her flesh and blood that she could overlook the growing rift between them that these changes represented. But it was a rift she could bridge with her memories, and she was determined that it would never grow so wide that she couldn't reach him.

For most of the year she could only guess at what was happening to him, but when he returned the changes were always enough to cause her surprise. In as many years as there were fingers on her hands, she saw him grow from little boy to adolescent to young man. One year, he was a full head taller than she. The next time, his voice had changed. The following year he returned only long enough to tell her he was leaving. War had broken out on the other side of the world and he was going to help the Americans fight, he said. She could do nothing, except to prepare a medicine pouch for sacred corn pollen and protection amulets to ensure his safe return.

Then her world descended into unrelenting silence.

Sometimes, as she followed the sheep, her mind wandered, and she wouldn't be following the flock of old ewes out in the desert, but would be far off in a strange green land where he fought for the *bilagáanaas* who had taken him from her. Sometimes the loneliness was overwhelming and tears rolled down her cheeks. She lived in a strange world where everything revolved around her, but she was desperately alone. Eventually she lost track of days, months, and sometimes, she thought, years. But even in the silence of her world, she clung to her memories. She drew on them like hardy plants draw on the deep, unseen waters of the desert for sustenance.

II.

She hardly slept at all that night. He was coming home. The sheer weight of that fact made her toss and turn on her narrow bed until she had to get up. She went out sometime after midnight and looked up at the night sky. The constellations and countless bright stars twinkled like jewels, and the wide hazy band of the Milky Way arched overhead like a luminescent spine. Somewhere off to the west, a lone coyote howled.

In the morning she went out again just as the sun broke through a thick bank of clouds hanging over the mountains to the east. Long shafts of sunlight probed the myriad folds and creases of the land around her. She breathed deeply of the invigorating morning air and felt so buoyant that she sang. The sheep bleated from the corral when they saw her, but she had more important things to do. They would have to wait. She put on her seldom-worn velveteen blouse, the glossy red one with decorative buttons made of shiny American coins. Then she combed back her hair and fastened it into a tight knot that pulled the skin of her face tautly across her cheekbones. It had been a long time since she'd last put on her silver-and-turquoise jewelry, but this was an occasion that called for nothing but the best. She sipped a cup of coffee while she waited for her neighbors who were going to take her to the trading post. The trader had sent word that her grandson would be arriving on the monthly supply truck.

She had just finished the coffee when she heard the distant whinny of a horse, and then just barely, the faint, lilting voice of a man singing. As the wagon drew nearer, there was the jingle of harnesses and the creak of wooden wheels. She went out and closed the door behind her. The neighbor's wife was sitting in the box of the wagon with her two daughters all wrapped up in their finest shawls. This was an an occasion for them, too. She climbed into the back of the wagon and settled down for the long ride to the post.

They unharnessed the horses near the post and kindled a fire. Her neighbor left to join a group of other men gambling under the shade of the trees surrounding the post, while she and his wife set about fixing their noon meal. She secretly scrutinized the neighbor's daughters to see if either one of them might make a suitable wife for her grandson. But she saw that they spent too much time idling and fussing with their clothes. They sat in the shade of the wagon while their mother made bread and cooked meat over the hot coals. No, she thought, they would not do.

They ate slowly, watching the comings and goings at the post. Shadows evaporated in the heat as the sun took hold of the land. Heat waves danced above the dunes and plain, while overhead buzzards wheeled lazily in the rising thermals. Eventually, the time for the arrival of the truck drew near. She kept herself busy helping the neighbor's wife with this and that, so they wouldn't see how anxious she really was. Later, she visited with the people gathered under the long wooden porch, laughing and jesting with them good-naturedly. A feeling of expectation charged the air. Frequent glances were cast down the dirt road that wound out of the valley. Suddenly, there was a shout; the truck had been sighted. She straightened her shawl and smoothed her skirt.

The truck pulled up to the post in a cloud of dust and some of the men rose to help the trader unload his supplies. They hefted boxes of tins, iron tools, bolts of bright cloth and numerous bundles—but they might as well have been old sheepskins. *Where is he?* she wondered, and then she saw him. He stepped down from the cab of the truck and stretched. He scanned the crowd casually, and toward the rear he saw her. She made her way through the crowd and quietly embraced him. He saw that her eyes brimmed with tears and he felt embarrassed. "Yá'át'ééh," he said, and gently grasped her hand. Then the neighbors stepped forward with hearty greetings and proffered hands. The two girls were suddenly coy. The people looked at him, at how the medals pinned to the front of his uniform glinted in the sun. He was tall and handsome, and someone speculated—by his appearance—who his father might have been. The two girls tried to capture his attention with their finery and affected coyness. She had never been so happy in her life. He had come home at last.

A wild storm broke not long after they had started for home, and they were soaked. The horses bent to the wheels, but the road was muddy and sudden rivers of brown storm water blocked their way. The fine shawls bled their colors and the girls were bedraggled. Then just before they arrived at the *hooghan*, the rain abated and a brilliant rainbow appeared in the mist under the immense gray belly of the storm cloud.

The lamp flickered as a moth dropped down into the chimney of the lamp and spun inside in agony. Her breath caught in her throat as an image flashed through her mind: in slow motion, a figure in khaki green metamorphosed into a twisted mass. The moth beat frantically against the glass, but it was trapped hopelessly and soon burst into flame.

Several years after he left for the *bilagáanaa's* war, a crew of men had come marching across the valley and left behind a row of stakes driven into the ground, marking the path of a highway that would soon cut the valley in two. She saw the road as a further sign of the assault on her world. Like a deadly and efficient predator, the road soon began exacting a heavy toll on the life of the valley. The shells of innumerable insects and carcasses of animals soon littered the sides of the pavement. Only the scavengers found reason to rejoice, or so she imagined as she watched the unremitting carnage. In her mind's eye, the world was gripped in chaos.

The morning he returned, he got up before daybreak. She heard him stir the ashes through the grate inside the stove. Soon, there was the familiar roar of the fire rising up the stovepipe. He went out and watched the sun rise from atop a nearby hill.

As she peeled potatoes for breakfast, she noticed that he was ill at ease. He fidgeted, clasping and unclasping his hands. He stared listlessly into space and nodded vaguely at things she said, and she wondered what it was that beckoned so strongly. The potatoes spattered and sizzled as she dumped them into the hot grease. He looked at her then, his attention focused entirely on her seemingly for the first time since he'd been back. He saw an old woman, brown as a piñon nut and weathered like an old tree. She was his grandmother and she had raised him, but something had changed, and she felt as if he were looking at her through someone else's eyes.

He'd been away many years and he had seen and done many things. He had experienced firsthand the *bilagáanaas'* world, seen their marvelous inventions and the awesome power of their weapons. He had seen their bustling cities and tasted of their food and their women, sailed around the earth and seen it from thirty thousand feet up. But he had learned, too, of his inferior place in that world. And it was with that experience that he looked at her now, as a *bilagáanaa* might look at an old Indian woman, through a barrier of words and things. He saw a wizened squaw frying potatoes for breakfast in an old ramshackle *hooghan* out in the middle of nowhere.

They ate in silence and he watched her, acutely aware of the way she ate. He saw that she had only a few teeth left and had trouble eating. Her face was deeply wrinkled and wisps of gray hair stuck in the air like antennae. He was surprised that he could distance himself from her like that and look at her so coldly, so flatly.

She wiped the dishes off carefully and put them away after they'd done eating, then sat down. She wanted to talk to him about a few things now that he was back, about how tradition dictated certain things, namely, taking a wife and settling down. *Iiná*—life—was the thing. He listened to her low voice and remembered when he could hear her yell from a long ways off. The new voice made him feel cheated. It was a fragile, hollowed-out shell of what had once been. A sharp undercurrent of loss cut at him and he felt something give way, some fundamental support collapse into a tumult of emotion. He felt the change so intensely that he wanted to leave the room.

At school all they had talked about was about becoming something, a carpenter, a plumber, a mechanic, an electrician—anything, as long as it fit in with their design. But now here she was, sounding like he was back for good. Here she was, making plans and telling him things that didn't matter, that couldn't possibly fit in with what he'd learned to want. He felt something crack open within him. He saw it clearly. He was an outsider in the *bilagáanaa* world, would always be, as hard as he tried to fit in. As he listened to her, he realized too, that he could not stay.

After a few days, he left with the excuse that he was going to the trading post, but he kept going until he found himself sitting at a dingy table inside a dark bordertown bar. Through a haze of alcohol and cigarette smoke he caught a glimpse of himself in a bar mirror and flinched. He wondered what he was doing there, but he couldn't answer that, so he just ordered another drink. He could not bring himself to go back to the old woman's place in this condition and face the disappointment in her eyes. He would wait, he decided, maybe tomorrow, maybe the next day, he didn't know.

The sudden appearance of her grandson, drunk at her door after two weeks' absence, startled and shocked her, but she bit back the hurt and tears long enough to leave the *hooghan*. She sat down in the dirt under the arbor and listened to him moving around inside. She slumped with the grief, remembering the day long ago when she had sat there with a fistful of dirt scooped from his footprints. She remembered her fervent prayers that he would return to her whole, unaffected by the influences of the *bilagáanaa's* world. *"Shee'awéé,"* she whispered, as she scooped up a fistful of dirt and let it sift through her fingers.

Later, when she went back inside, he was snoring loudly on the cot. The smell of alcohol nauseated her, but she covered him with her quilt. She knew that she would accept this change in him, just as she had accepted all the other changes he had wrought in her world. He was, after all, her flesh and blood.

III.

The highway tops a hill before it winds past the bar. At certain times of day, traffic flows along it so thick that it forms near-solid lines. At dusk and into the night, thousands of headlights come on and fuse into long glittering strings of light that follow the rise and fall of the hills, skirting allotted lands and leaping over deep arroyos in steel bridges.

Not long after the highway had snaked through the valley, a square cinderblock building had appeared beside the road. It was a bar, and soon a ragtag queue of hollow-eyed men and women, distracted from their tasks and lives, haunted its periphery. He found himself frequently among their ranks, pressed up against the rough blocks like a cold fly on a wall.

Once, while sharing a bottle with someone on the hill behind the bar, a terrifying vision had struck him: the headlights on the highway below coalesced into a glittering, solid body—a snake of light. He saw it coil, rear up, and strike at him, and he scuttled blindly backward. "Hey *shi*-buddy!" His friend shook him. "Take it easy. Calm down, *héi, shi*-boy. You're awright." Even then, his heart took a while to slow down. In his mind he saw the glowing snake with heat-seeking, malefic eyes coming toward him.

It was starkly cold, that winter night. His foot kept catching on things and he stumbled and tried to steady himself, but the earth whirled and spun. He collapsed in the tall grass and weeds lining the highway and pulled a bottle from his pants. He took a swig, gagged, but kept it down. He rose to his feet unsteadily and looked to the crest of the hill to see if any cars were coming. He was bone-tired and sick and wanted only to go home. The old woman would let him in, he knew, even as she scolded him for being drunk again. He looked to the top of the hill once more.

Nothing stirred in the night, and the sky was full of incredible beauty, countless stars that winked and glinted in the crystalline air.

He lurched awkwardly onto the highway, swaying with each step. His feet dragged and the earth reeled. His shoe caught on a crack in the pavement and he went crashing. His face hit the pavement with a slap and blood spurted from his nose. He closed his eyes against the detonation of lights in his vision. He trembled uncontrollably as the ground spun and the darkness descended. He pressed his cheek against the warm pavement and drew his knees up like a baby. He lay huddled there. Then, dimly, he became aware of a sound. What it was and where it came from, he couldn't tell. All he could make out was that it was growing. Strangely, he felt nothing. Not cold, not fear, nothing at all. It was as if he had become detached from his body.

The sound grew, sending vibrations through the chilly air. Suddenly, a pair of headlights appeared at the top of the hill, and then another, and another. They grew into a long string of lights that descended sinuously down the hill. He opened his eyes and stared impassively as the snake with glittering eyes came sliding inexorably toward him. At the last moment, he closed his eyes.

The driver of the first car didn't see anything at first, then a dim shape on the road, but he could not stop. Like a silent scream, brake lights flared and bathed the night with a bloody glow. The line of cars did not stop until several of them had passed over him. In the darkness and silence of the aftermath, there was the sound of a woman sobbing. "We didn't see. We just didn't see."

The old woman shuddered and stirred from her thoughts. The room had grown cool and the stove was silent. She brushed her face to shoo away the moths that fluttered there, but finding tears instead, rubbed them between her fingertips. She got up slowly from her chair and blew out the lamp. She felt her way to her bed with her feet and sat down wearily. In the morning she would take out the sheep and follow them into the valley, moving from one clump of greasewood to another, seeking the scant shelter they offered from the chilling wind. The day after that would be no different.

At last, she lay down and closed her eyes.

Squatters

The town lies in a narrow valley bounded by tilted red sandstone hogbacks to the east, blue mountain ridges to the south, and yellow piñon- and juniper-covered hills to the west and north. The sun is a hot white disk in the pure blue sky. In the tangle of saplings and brush shading a narrow wash behind Tomada's store is a hut made of cardboard, and inside it are a man and a woman. The woman sits upright and the man is prone and motionless. A beam of sunlight reaches through a thin gap in the roof and falls on her face. Her countenance is haggard, full of hollows and creases, though she is not yet old.

Her brown eyes merely reflect the incoming light and add nothing of their own. This in contrast to the luminescence that had filled them before when the man lying beside her had

211

laughed, had said the one thing that pleased her most, had touched her in the special way that she liked: his big hands gentle, his rough fingers the brush of wingtips on her face, and his voice, low, murmuring, *"Áazhinee' asdząą. Háádéé'sha' shaayíníyá?"*

She caresses his face, but he is not aware of her touch. Beads of sweat glitter on his forehead. Though it is sweltering, he shakes as if with cold. He moans and shudders. She sighs and momentarily ceases sweeping her hand over his face to keep away the buzzing flies. She looks down and whispers, *"Alhosh, hastiin."* Then she looks away and resumes the mechanical fanning motion. She will sit there forever, if need be.

She has not slept for some time. She has seen the sun and the stars wheel across the sky again and again. Her eyes stay open, but they see nothing beyond the visions whirling in her mind. Chaos is loose in this special place, in this haven he had prepared for her, where they had camped ever since the cops told them to get off the streets or else.

She sits patient as stone in the noon heat as the land teems with heat waves. Her hand stirs a meager ripple in the air. Their sole luxury is a foam mattress found in a nearby field. He lies on that, loose-limbed, moaning now and then. He needs help, but she cannot will herself to leave his side even for a moment. She remains firmly rooted, brushing away flies, staring all the while into the air that swims with secret images.

The man behind the counter in the store knows they are there. He watches closely. He regards them as squatters, though they are camped on a patch of no-man's-land in the wash marking the rear boundary of his property. He knows they have been there for some time, scavenging from the dumpster behind his store and others nearby. He never caught them at it, but he knows.

Once, lately, he found himself caught in a dilemma: whether or not to throw out a perfectly good loaf of week-old

212

bread, a partial crate of overripe fruit, or whatever. But he came to his senses in time and shook that notion out of his head. Whatever had possessed him to even consider? It would be too much like he was condoning their wretched existence.

It isn't his fault that they are there. They merely have gotten what they deserve, hanging around town without any money or legitimate business. If they really wanted to, they could go back to wherever the hell they are from. Surely they have someplace—surely they have someone. With that, the man finds it easier not to feel sorry. They are perfectly capable of walking to the highways leading out of town and out of his mind.

He discovered their presence behind his store not long after the hut appeared in the weeds and young Siberian elms crowding the wash. He investigated right away, poking his head into the dim interior. He saw it was surprisingly tidy. There was a yellowed foam mattress on the clean-swept earthen floor and a small sack suspended from the branch holding up the roof. He knocked down the sack and was amused and repulsed by the things that fell out: a quarter carcass of a barbequed chicken, a partially eaten microwave burrito, and some stale potato chips. He snorted. *Ladrones*, that's what they were. Thieves. Freeloaders.

He kept a look out for their return. When he knew they were back, he stormed out and told them to get the hell off his property or he would call the police. They responded with glum stares. "What's the matter with you people," he shouted into their silent faces, "living like animals, rummaging through my garbage for food? *Cabrones*! Don't you have any pride?"

They just stood there looking at him. "Do you hear me?" he shouted again. "Well, you can't live here anymore." With that, he turned and kicked at the cardboard. But he wasn't prepared for what happened. He didn't realize just how flimsy the structure was. He was genuinely surprised when it collapsed. He stood there gaping as the cardboard folded in

213

on itself and dust motes boiled up. When he finally turned around, they were gone.

He saw them again a few days later, sitting in the shade of saplings several hundred feet up the wash. Every day thereafter, they moved closer and closer until they returned to the spot where their hut had been. He looked back there one morning and saw, but he didn't bother to yell. They'd only stare dumbly and annoy him with their silence. Because of his blood pressure, the only sensible thing to do was to ignore them as much as possible. And though he would never admit it, his bare tolerance for them has gradually become something like a proprietary interest in their whereabouts. It has become something of a ritual to glance in their direction as he takes out the trash in the mornings.

She is patient and keeps up her vigil, fanning away the persistent flies. None of them will have a chance to land. As vigilant as she is, however, her motions are listless. Without his voice to lead or cheer her, she is lost. She can only sit there fanning away flies. He is tall and slight of build, ordinary-looking perhaps, but he is good to her. She leans forward slightly and whispers. At one time he was an imposing figure, she knows, because of the way he carried himself: head high, shoulders back. She was content to remain in the background and admire the way he had with people.

"K'aalógii." The first time he called her by that name she had blushed. Butterfly. Elegant dark limbs and lustrous wings, perched on a trembling blue trumpet, proboscis unfurling, dipping into nectar. She sighs, overcome with the memory: the star-strewn sky, the fragrant grass, the sound of crickets, and the weight of him gently crushing her as his breath burned on her neck. She'd lain quietly next to him afterward, listening to his breathing and feeling the cool night air move over her body.

But then he groans. She tugs at his shoulders and slowly turns him on his side as he succumbs to a fit of coughing.

214

In the muted light, the hard lines on his face are erased. He looks young again, and she finds herself answering his moans with those of her own.

She hadn't suspected, even when her menses had stopped. The pain and blood had come one night without warning. In the morning she carried the bloody rags into the hills and buried the bundle under a large juniper tree. He didn't ask about her long silences afterward, but now and then he gently touched the back of his hand against her cheek. Wings. He couldn't have known she was sick until she collapsed. He had run into the streets and flagged down a squad car. And when the ambulance came, he had climbed in and held her hand.

She woke to the frown of a *bilagáanaa* nurse peering over thick bifocals as she dabbed and wiped. "Lord knows, it could be for the best," the nurse said. "There are far too many unfortunate children in this world as it is." Afterward, a doctor explained that she could no longer have children. She had waited too long and infection had set in. She turned away and closed her eyes. When she opened them later, she saw that he was sitting there on the chair beside her bed. *"Haalá nít'é?"* he asked, but she could not speak.

She drifted in and out of a fog for days, calling the names of people he did not know. *"Hadesbaa'* . . . *Adzáá lichíí'* . . . *Hastiin nééz."* Then one day she could focus on the underbellies of clouds through the window. A few days later she followed him out into the glare of the noon sun and trailed slowly after him as he walked down the hill from the hospital. She felt weak and empty. She could say nothing, but her eyes drank in the sweep of the land. As she looked, she was filled with an intense longing. The feeling ballooned inside her until with a shock she realized that she was lifting. She was floating right over his head. She rose high over the town and the surrounding hills, over the flat dry plains beyond and onward toward the distant blue mountains. She skimmed over the rocky foothills and higher up onto the lushly forested summit, where the wind moved among the pines and the air was thickly scented with the smell of growing things. Water rippled in ponds and lakes. Blue lupins and red Indian paintbrush, colorful butterflies, iridescent birds and insects, all vied for her eye, and she abandoned herself to the sensations.

He should see this, she thought. *Nizhóní*. So peaceful. That's when she realized her mistake. She felt the water-soft grip of his voice wrap around her. *"Áhál'áanee' asdzáá, shaanéíndzá."* She felt his words begin to pull her back, bit by bit, until with a loud wail she hurtled back over the endless and precious land—out of control—and dropped sobbing from the sky back into his solid arms.

The man in the store feels strangely agitated and paces back and forth behind the counter, stroking his dark mustache. He blames the coffee for his restlessness and drums his fingers on the countertop, grimly staring at the closed-circuit TV monitor by the register. He wordlessly tends to the wild-eyed Sunday customers who come into the store with piles of change for bottles of cologne and mouthwash.

She dabs the spittle from his lips with the hem of her skirt and in the same motion wipes his glistening forehead. He grinds his teeth and shivers. After a while, she puts his head onto her lap and begins to croon a melody she remembers from somewhere. Traffic drones in the background. A group of schoolchildren pass in front of the store, laughing and chattering with high-pitched voices. He sighs deeply and stops shivering. The grasshoppers go quiet. She looks down. His face is so beautiful and peaceful that her heart clenches.

Precisely at that moment a car backfires, startling a flock of birds from a nearby tree. They circle overhead once, filling the air with the commotion of a sudden wind, and fly away to the north. She leans forward and kisses him. She touches his hair and strokes his face. At last, she gets up and walks to the front of the store, where the storekeeper sees her standing.

He comes out immediately and tells her to move on, but the way she looks at him stops him in his tracks. "Go on now," he says. "You and your friend both." But she merely stares like she doesn't see him at all. "Go on now," he repeats. "I'll go roust your friend. This time I don't want you coming back, you hear?" He walks around to the back of the store and slowly approaches the hut.

He hears the buzzing of the flies before he actually sees them. What he sees in the hut makes him step back quickly. He stumbles across the wash. "Jesus," he says. His mind cannot shake the image, the emaciated body crawling with flies. He runs around the corner, meaning to grab the woman and call the police, but when he looks up and down the street it is as motionless as at dawn.

August

The boughs and branches of the forest bent with
the weight of water droplets that formed continuously from the
moisture in the air and the misting low clouds which
overwhelmed the sun for four days in a row until the land was
soaked and could absorb no more and shed the rain as it fell
so that streams sloughed off hillsides and meadows in wide
rippling sheets across clearings which were funnels for the
water that beseiged yet cleaned the land including the three
stark white tipis that rose among the pines at the edge of the
clearing where songs and prayers would ring out at dusk
though for now it was so quiet and only the hiss of gentle rain
was heard until late afternoon when water drums and gourd
rattles rose above the murmur of voices and laughter as some
of the men practiced for the night-long service that would end

219

at daybreak with a feast which the women were busy preparing even as children pestered and complained and galloped around as if they smelled the special freedom like horses scent water but the cooks only smiled with patience and indulgence as small brown hands grabbed tidbits off tabletops while they reveled in the congeniality of gossip and food and gestured with flour-speckled hands which provided exclamation marks as explosive mirth bubbled up when someone told a good one about the lost tourist and the reservation gingerbread man or the even better one about the old days and rain and women and salamanders which left them in stitches waving their hands helplessly until cramps quelled them long enough to overhear the conversations outside of young people talking about rock and hiphop and the baddest bands and hairstyles and so forth as the afternoon leaned into dusk when fires were lit inside the tipis which then glowed like Chinese lanterns or shadow theaters that kept the children busy guessing who was which shape on the stretched canvas until they grew sleepy and drifted off to their beds and the fire chief stoked a fire that would burn all night with unbridled power rising up to console and inflame with allusions to warmth and the sun shining fierce as hope or the blazing stars which had it been clear they might have glimpsed through the smoke hole where the poles were tied together into a brace strong enough to withstand high winds though that wouldn't happen everyone said as they dressed in fine clothes and jewelry and hats and hairdos that were in style like woven vests and ropers and silver and nugget turquoises that would gleam in the flickering firelight as the services commenced with drumbeats and tobacco and feelings of goodwill like cedar incense upon the assembled as they leaned forward in earnest prayer or just gazed into the dancing flames and the glowing bed of embers banked against the low altar of sand laid down and tamped into a long narrow crescent that held a single line representing life drawn across the top from end to end above the mottled gray-and-black holy bird of ashes that filled the hollow of the crescent and mimicked the pattern on someone's Pendleton robe or Hudson Bay jacket which also echoed the gray of embers and the muted night infused with good thoughts and songs and prayers until without warning a woman screamed and stood up shaking out her shawl exclaiming how cold had been the thing that grazed her hand and the excitement spread and soon they were stuffing their fine Pendletons into the narrow openings along the bottom of the tipis to keep out the wriggling intruders whose translucent or buff or gray bodies alarmed them maybe on account of the joke about rain and women and salamanders or maybe because of the way they looked moving about in the dancing firelight like alligators crouching low and hissing and arching their backs.

The Blood Stone

The plane rumbles down the runway, past weeds and grass and patches of bare earth. It climbs in a noisy arc around the granite cliffs and spires of the Sandias and begins the long journey over flatness. Snow-splotched mountains to the north and west dissolve in the haze, and the land turns from brown to green.

Hózhó naashá dooleel, hózhó 'íishlaa dooleel. Áyaa díishjí hózhó naashá, 'áyaa díishjí hózhó íshlaa.

I am rising on a sunbeam, traveling on a rainbow. I am going to meet my father the Sun. I am holy with pollen. I am dressed in sacred jewels. Far to the west, *Tsoodzil*, sacred mountain, passes, a mere anthill. *Yéi'iitsoh* is dead, his blood congealed, solidified black. El Malpais.

223

"Complimentary snack, sir?" I shake my head. The smell of peanuts drifts in the cabin.

I am approaching the house of the Sun, steeling myself for the tests to confirm my identity, when she returns.

"Would you care for a drink?" I look up and see my brown face reflected in her blue eyes.

"Some white wine, please." I reach into my pocket and scoop coins and bills onto the tray. A spot of red gleams amid the the dull coins and crumpled bills. "Is that jasper?" She smiles, setting down my glass.

"No, it's just an ordinary stone." As if it is an ordinary thing, carrying stones.

"Well, it's pretty."

The plane tips slightly to turn. Sunlight flashes on the wine and stone. The stone glows like a live coal.

"*Díí nani'á dooleel, shitsoóí.*" I hear the words distinctly, as if they have been whispered in my ear.

"*La'í gó hane' hóló ndi, la' bee dasína lá,*" she says. Hank Williams is singing about being so lonesome. Flames crackle in the barrel stove. A coffee can of sage and water perfumes the room with steam. The stone nestles in the cup of her upturned hand like a drop of blood. It is egg-shaped, shiny, deep red with hints of copper. She closes her fist on it, curling her yellow-nailed thumb over gnarled fingers. She is motionless for several moments, staring into her lap. Then she grasps my wrist. She shakes my hand flat and drops the stone onto my palm.

"*Díí nani'á,*" she says, folding my fingers over it. I nod that I will.

"*Nichei yée sheiní'á nt'éé'.*" She smiles. The old man, her father, is twenty years dead. I hadn't thought about him in a long time. Now he steps into my mind. Tall, ruddy, red-haired and blue-eyed in a land of brown-skinned, black-haired people.

"*Eii hwééldi gó na'isdee' yéedáá' nízhdii'á, jiní.*" She points with her lips at my closed fist. The stone is warm from her touch.

I remember the pictures I'd seen of the people huddled in brush shelters at Fort Sumner. They are ragged and thin. I am surprised to see that my thumb is rubbing the stone.

She is an archive. Countless nights we listened to her telling, captivated by the scenes she painted with her words. The ordinary land we knew, the desert, the mountains, the plains, transformed into a place where magic prevailed and monsters prowled.

There had been four worlds before this one, and this, the fifth world, the Glittering World, is the final one. Each of the previous worlds ended in cataclysm, its destruction brought about by the inhabitants. This time, *lahgo naahwidoodáál*. A whole new existence we cannot imagine. No one knows except the Holy People, and they are keeping it a secret. Another emergence. *Hajíínéí*, when we emerged as *Diné*, and the Twins undertook the journey to meet their father, the Sun. Carrying with them weapons of lightning and rainbows to do battle with *Yéi'iitsoh*, the Giant. They rode into the sky on sunbeams and rainbows.

This is what the land must have looked like from their vantage point in the sky, I think. *Sisnaajiní*, an anthill. And the land an archetypal tapestry, a work of brown and green and yellow and white.

Thin streamers of vapor swirl off the polished wings as we skim through clouds. Sunlight glints on the slick surfaces, on dents and rivets. Clouds pass like trees.

Hajíínéí. I do not question it. Her words are confident, rich with nasal tones, clicks, and glottal stops. *"Alk'idáá' jiní,"* she says. A long time ago—ancient, magical words. She stops frequently to spit into the can she keeps by her bed. She does this with deliberation, so much a part of the telling. Long silences punctuate her stories, and we drift into the world of her words. Then she shifts on her bed and the squeak of the springs is a summons.

"Nichei yéé ániinee," she says. She reaches into her flour sack of belongings. She puts a pinch of Skoal inside her cheek. The mole on her eyebrow bobs as her parchment lids blink. She puckers her lips and spits into the can. The clock on the table across the room ticks. A moth whirs around the kerosene lamp. Her calico cat leaps onto the tabletop and swats at the moth. *"Doo áhályáada, héi!"* She mutters with a shake of her head. Crazy thing.

I wait for her to continue the telling. The cat comes and purrs on her lap. Her hands caress it absently.

"Nichei yée ániinee'—"

A small boy is alone in the white sun. Sheep nibble on saltbush in the broad wash below. The only sounds are the tinkle of their bells and the occasional bleat of a lamb. A hawk circles overhead, dips, flaps higher, veers off to the north. The boy sings in a high-pitched voice. *"Nich'i'lá hoogheé' ndi, nich'i'lá nízaad ndi . . ."* The words of the love song proclaim devotion of a sort he can't fully understand: The distance to your home may be far, and the journey arduous, but—

The sheep dog comes to him, wagging its tail.

"Nlish áhnidíshní."

Then the peace is shattered. *Hashkiiltsoóí*, his older brother, comes clattering down the rocky hillside. His horse is dark with sweat. Its chest heaves. There is green foam on the bit.

"Ti'!" shouts his brother. *"Bilagáanaa bigiizh déé' yinéél!"* The boy gasps. He pictures the soldiers spilling through the gap in the mountains.

His parents are waiting with four loaded packhorses. The cookfire is dead. A dark stain of grease on the ground buzzes with flies.

"Nóóda'í naalchi'í la' seeshí jiní." The broken body of the Ute scout had been found at the base of the cliffs lining the pass. The soldiers swarmed around it like angry ants. They are to be feared now more than ever. The packhorses toss their heads

226

and snort. His mother says nothing. The boy looks at the peach tree his father planted and turns away.

Two months later, in the dead of winter, they are staggering east. They cross the Rio Grande at Albuquerque and file past the twin bell towers of the mission. The Pueblo neophytes come out to stare silently at the long column of dead-eyed people moving past. A girl tries to stop a soldier from selling her newborn to the Spanish villagers and is killed. The boy screams at the sight of the girl's cleaved bloody skull. His mother faints and has to be carried by his father. The soldier returns and hacks off the head. Let this be a lesson. A scrawny dog drags it away, to the amusement of the soldiers. The boy cannot forget the sword for months afterward.

He learns to eat flour and beef on the arid plains, in a bend of the Pecos. They build the fort under guard and channel the river to irrigate their crops. There are plagues of grass-hoppers and worms and four years of drought. His father turns gaunt. His eyes grow vacant and he is unresponsive. In the spring of the fourth year, his mother's belly begins to grow, but there is no joy. At night, she thrashes and moans. He covers his ears not to hear, but he does anyway. *Dooda! Dooda!* She pleads with the hairy face looming over her, straining red, breathing liquor in her face. His father dies before the baby is born. After four days, his mother gathers rocks and piles them over the grave.

She keeps two things from that time; a red-haired, blue-eyed child, and a stone pried absentmindedly from the ground as they sit listening to the discussions about the treaty and the conditions of their release. The stone is red like blood and she tucks it into the waistband of her skirt. Now and then she takes it out. Gradually, it acquires a polish from her hands.

We hit turbulence and the plane shudders. We are between enormous thunderheads. Lightning leaps from cloud to cloud.

The masses flicker like strobes. The man across the aisle laughs at the antics of Bill Murray on the small monitor overhead.

"Why don't you have it polished and mounted on a chain?" Skye says. She is watering the ferns this morning. She has neglected them and their edges are brown. They are not things I'd keep in my apartment. She is like that: forgetful, self-absorbed, but kind otherwise.

"We've been over this before," I say.

"It's just that I think it would be safer, that's all." That's another thing about Skye. She is transparent. I know it bothers her. I have seen the expression on her face, tight, a put-on smile. She'd rather I let go the tangible evidence of my background. Be American. She doesn't understand.

"It would be like wearing my mother's head around my neck," I say. Streams of water pour from the hanging planters and she scurries for bowls and pans. I pour coffee and wait. She is not finished.

"You know what I mean," she says. "It'll get scratched, carrying it around in your pocket." She is exaggerating. The stone rarely travels with me. Most of the time it keeps my underwear company in the bureau. I know she contemplated theft—a friend snitched—but lost her nerve. How could she explain it when I have nothing worth stealing, least of all the stone? I know it scares her. It represents a part of my life that exists and will continue to exist without her. The stone must seem to her like a beating heart. Maybe I am wrong. The stone is after all only a chunk of—quartz? It may contain the skin oils of my direct ancestors, but do I consider my skin oils special blessings to pass on to my children?

"Jamie's friend asked about you." Skye wipes her hand on her T-shirt. "The anthropoid, I mean."

I smile. I can guess what's coming.

"He remembered you from the party. He told her about the way you had that little group in your palm. All you had to do was mention the stone." She bites her lip. It is an unconscious act. She looks wonderfully childlike. Her eyes search my face. What will I say? Will I compromise?

"Those anthropoids know the score," I say. They know how to namedrop. Chichen Itza. Machu Picchu. Chaco Canyon. I picture a pin drop in slow motion and bounce thunderously.

"That thing means more to you than . . ." She cannot finish the indictment. The coffee goes down like sand. I should explain this to her *Dinék'ehjí*, I think.

"*Yáadilá,*" I say. "It's just a stone."

"I'm sorry." She sits beside me. *Dinétah* and Boston, I think, oil and water. A breeze turns the ferns slowly. I see that her nails are painted the same color as the stone.

The plane slices through the clouds. The stone is in my pocket, hidden, and the man across the aisle snores. I flip up the tray and signal the flight attendant. There is a brief moment in which I imagine that I am approaching myself. I am naked but for breechcloth and paint. Feathers sprout from my head. I hold the stone like an orb. Sprigs of evergreens quiver on my wrists. I exude a wild, greasy smell. The snoring man twiches. My spear point is smeared with his blood.

"Yes, sir?" The attendant smiles. I give her my empty glass and watch her walk back down the aisle. Far below, Illinois natives see a pulsing red stone hurtling through the sky.

The old man is nearly bald, but his blue eyes are clear. He looks at me and laughs. "*Héiyee' ánít'í?*"

I identify myself. He thinks for a moment, sorting through progeny and relations. Then he nods. "*Áagi, áagi,*" He reaches out and grasps my clammy hand. I have come, boldly, to talk. Now I am at a loss. He waits, and I scratch one foot with the other. My knees poke through my jeans. He rests his hand on his cane. The pearl snaps on his western shirt gleam. His jeans are rolled up and a little toe sticks halfway out of one black sneaker.

"*Aa'?*"

I am startled. What does an eight-year-old kid have to talk about? I swallow. A chicken squawks outside. Other kids shout. He closes his eyes and asks after my mother, my link to him. She is fine and so are my siblings, but what I wanted to ask was—I falter. He is listening! "*Ha'át'íílá béé nílniih?*" A stupid question. What does he remember.

"*Da'hwééldi déé' ná'íldee' yéedáá?*" Yes, what was it like when they returned? *Hwééldi.* Fort Sumner.

I sit in the small sage-scented room all afternoon. He makes tea and shares his cache of graham crackers. I am full as I leave his house. I try to picture him as a child. Did he wonder about his father? Did he feel the tug of some land across the ocean in his dreams? Did he rage at the Holy People?

I pick at the chicken something on my plate, swimming in thin sauce. The sky flames yellow and orange and red as the sun drops below the horizon. The clouds glow like coral. Man-made constellations glimmer below. The man across the aisle licks his fingers.

"*Yáah,*" I say.

"Excuse me, sir." Those blue eyes again, that nonstop smile. "We're about to land. Please fasten your seat belt."

I have fallen asleep. The city's spectacular skyline is framed in the window; the red lights atop the skyscrapers blink. I click my belt into place and my fingers brush the stone. "*Kó náánéit'ash,*" I tell it. *Náánéit'ah yee'.*"

After the landing I walk down the corridor in a stream of chattering people. Eliseo shouts and hugs me. I laugh. We skirt regiments of yellow chairs and walk toward the escalator. He tells me about what has happened in my absence. Maria is sulking, he says, but he doesn't give a damn. She is getting too . . . too. He rolls his eyes. Ai, that woman!

"How was your trip?" he says finally, as we begin to slide down to the lower level.

"The folks are fine, bearing up well. I think they're relieved that she's gone, finally. You know what I mean?"

Eliseo nods. "Si."

"I'm glad that I took this." I take out the stone. There is a commotion behind us. I turn just as two guys come hurtling down the escalator and crash past, knocking the stone out of my hand. The stone bounces down the stairs and lands near the bottom. I watch as the stone drops between the moving teeth. Eliseo curses. An old woman above us moans. She has collapsed on the moving stairs. We are at her side in four steps. "My purse," she says. "They took it." Someone stops the escalator and I hold her hand. She is trembling. There is a flurry of activity. Security arrives and questions us. The thieves are long gone. I wait until the old woman is carried away on a stretcher. "Thank you," she says. "God bless you."

After they are gone, I fish the pouch of pollen from my luggage and ignoring stares and whispers sprinkle a pinch on the spot where the stone vanished. Then we leave. Outside, it is warm and the air vibrates with the din of the city. We are quiet during the long drive to my apartment. The streets are lively on this Saturday night.

"Tell me a tale," says Eliseo. "Something that'll help me deal with an angry woman."

"A tall order," I say, swirling the brandy in my glass.

"A long time ago, there was a young man. He was in love with a girl who lived on a hill across the valley. But there was no hope, he knew, because the girl's father did not approve. They could just ignore him and get together—that was done

231

a lot in those days—but the father's blessing meant much to him. So he plotted elaborate strategies and began raising a bride price. His neighbors raised their eyebrows. Who in their right mind would want *him*? Who who would want to subject themselves to ridicule and scorn? But love is unreasonable, if not indomitable.

"Finally the day comes that he has enough to offer for her hand. He dresses in his best velveteen shirt and brand-new Levis, concho belt, silver-and-turquoise bracelets, bowguard, rings, strands of coral-and-turquoise beads, and turquoise nuggets dangling from his ears. He is magnificent. At least he thinks so, as he sets out on his best horse outfitted with his best saddle and trimmings. He practices what he will say as he ascends the hill to her home. A pack of mangy dogs charge at the top and bark and nip at the horse's hooves. They halt near the ramada. He feigns confidence, but a bead of sweat rolls down the side of his face. He wipes it quickly and clears his throat. Nothing happens. He blows his nose loudly, holding it between his fingers. Still nothing. He hacks and spits. Then he does it, tosses decorum out the window.

" *'Yá'át'ééh,'* he says, his voice higher than he'd intended.

" *'Yóoweh di nani ch'íidii!'* he is told. Get the hell away from here. He feels his heart curl like a sun-dried peach.

"He cannot go home, so he builds a fire over the lava rocks at the sweat lodge. He strips and sprawls in the sand. What is wrong with me, he wonders, looking at his naked limbs. He slams his fist into the sand. He is pale as a lizard's belly where the sun has not browned him, and his pubic hair blazes orange. He moans and tears at the hair on his chest and belly, but the pain brings him to his senses. He goes into the sweat lodge and sings. His songs are soaring hope.

"He does not go to her home again; instead, he throws himself into numbing physical labor. His mother's homestead, where he still lives, is transformed. Corrals spring out of the ground, two new *hooghan* appear. Her ramada, where she sits most days, is the envy of the local women. The livestock aren't neglected, either. The horses ripple and shine, the cattle bear fine calves, and his mother loses none of her sheep. The local men cannot help but notice. Maybe there is something to this guy, they think.

"The girl, too, has been watching. As the days pass, her resolve grows until finally one day she packs her belongings. Her father blusters and threatens—You'll have freaks! He'll poison you with his blue eyes! You'll get sick lying with that bilagáanaa!—but she doesn't listen. She walks down the hill one evening and appears out of the growing dusk as he sits outside smoking and contemplating the day. He leaps to his feet. They do not speak. They do not need to."

"Maybe Maria isn't so bad, after all," Eliseo says. "Maybe I'll give her another chance." He is jealous because she spoke to a stranger at the KC dance.

After Eliseo leaves, the apartment lapses into silence. I wander through the rooms. I am for a moment on the balcony. There is a breeze and it seems to fan the lights of the city. The sound of traffic is tedious. I do not answer the phone, though it rings and rings. I open the bureau drawer. For a moment my hand rests on the cloth inside, in the hollow where the stone once lay. Finally, I smooth over the depression and click on the lamp.

Tomorrow, Eliseo and Maria will drop by with an offering— a casserole, some wine or something. Eliseo will pretend that nothing happened, that he never said anything abut Maria.

And maybe, if they behave, I will tell another story.

The Hyatt, the Maori, and the Yanamamo

After supper, I cut a slice of watermelon and sat on the porch steps, spitting seeds and watching the shadow of the mountains behind my home lean across the valley. As it touched the horizon, there was a final smolder of color. The pale cliffs of Chaco Canyon gleamed like inlays of mica on the edge of the world. Gray thunderheads tinged with orange and pink glowed over Torreón and the Sierra Nacimiento. They were Holy People come from the south, dressed in icy robes of water. They had come in answer to our prayers once again, bringing nothing less than life itself.

Anaa'sází. I imagined the canyon sacred with the jingle of copper bells, vibrant with voices, bright with parrot feathers. The Ancient Ones dancing. Prayer in motion. The plaza at Pueblo Bonito awash with firelight and the thunder of drums

235

rolling like waves through the canyon. Far to the east, a rainbow glowed in the last light.

Áhálááneeʼ, I thought. How better to express the joy and awe?

I sank into the deep cushions of the sofa and the indigo landscape outside dropped below the cluttered sill. A gilded dragon. Brass elephants. A pair of rosy-cheeked youth, a boy and girl caught in midstride, a wooden bucket held between them. They had been on their way back from the well when the ceramist froze them for all time. I aimed the remote and the television came alive, hissing.

Thunderous applause. Hysterical laughter. Then tight faces as Eddie Murphy began talking about black and white. Uneasy laughter. Then the dog barked. I punched the mute button and the gate hinges squeaked twice. There was a knock on the door. I flicked on the porch light and Frank, my neighbor and in-law, squinted in the sudden glare. He stepped quickly into the room, trailing a faint wake of rain scent. His expression was grim.

"Don't tell me," I said. "Is she—"

"She is," he nodded. "Again."

While I rummaged for flashlights in the kitchen drawers, he told me that he had just got back from pulling a cow out of the mud at the watering hole. "That took me all afternoon and then I come home to this mess," he said, shaking his head. "Shit." He'd left the oldest girl in charge, but she'd been too busy gabbing on the phone to notice anything.

The last time the old lady had disappeared, they found her huddled in a clump of saltbush, cold, hungry, and nearly dehydrated.

A knotted cord, images and emotions, slipped through my mind: the old lady—my grandfather's sister—crawling on hands and knees through the furnace heat of a summer day. Over scorching sand, through fields of tumbleweeds, over anthills, under barbwire fences, across arroyos and the busy bus road.

I pictured the thick calluses on her palms, and her face, darkened by the sun, seamed with wrinkles like the eroded foothills to the west. Her failing eyes, clouded and blinking behind thick glasses. Gray hair, once glossy black, in disarray, loosened in wisps from the woolen hair tie. And carrying on conversations with men and women long dead.

One time I had come across her crouching in a shallow ditch, cowering in terror. *"Yíiyá, shiyázhí,"* she'd whispered. *"Naakaai dashooltse' lágo."* There hadn't been any Mexican horsemen in the area for over three hundred years.

We walked slowly, swinging the beams of our flashlights back and forth. Voices called out now and then. *"Shimá sání! Shimá sání!"* Grandmother, grandmother. Some of the children whispered and giggled, but an adult voice hushed them. We might not see her, you carrying on like that.

It was impossible to see anything besides the stars overhead and the flashlights bobbing in the darkness. In a few minutes, a pair of headlights swung out from the cluster of our houses and bounced toward us. There was no road, so the vehicle maneuvered around sandhills and clumps of rabbitbrush. The long beams lit up the rugged slopes of the foothills a mile away.

"There she is!" someone shouted.

"Shimá sání!"

"No, it's a piece of wood, you dorks."

From the top of a low outcrop of clay, the headlights reached across the plain. The vehicle backed up slowly and swept its beams over the land. Then it descended and came toward us. Grace, who was Frank's wife and my aunt, pulled up next to me in their truck. She rolled down her window and motioned to me. I went over, but she didn't say anything for a while. She stared out the windshield.

"You must think I'm awful," she said.

"No, Grace, I don't."

The truth was that I didn't, really. I understood more than she seemed to suppose. I waited. A burrowing owl called out, predicting more warm weather. A movement at the side caught my eye. "This flashlight of yours burned out," Frank said, handing me the cold object. I clicked it on and the filament in the bulb glowed a dull orange.

"I don't think we'll find her tonight," Frank said. "Best thing's to start again in the morning. Right now, she's holed up somewhere. We won't find her like that."

"You sure?" I asked, but I knew he was right. She would be too afraid to move. She would hide.

Grace sighed and pulled a tissue from the box on the dashboard. "It's sure as hell not easy," she said, her eyes glittering in the dim light from the instrument panel. Frank shifted uneasily and looked away. He leaned against the cab. I excused myself to tell the others. As I walked away, I heard the truck door open.

"Sometimes I feel like quitting my job, but . . ." Grace said back at her house, waving her hand vaguely about the room as she poured coffee. I knew all about their situation and could sympathize. Splinters and stone—that was rez life. Many families had gone to find better times in the cities, and those who stayed behind were left with the weight of holding things together. Frank and Grace had seven mouths to feed. And if that wasn't enough, the old lady had gone steadily downhill for a couple of years.

She'd cut quite a figure in her youth—a term I once heard her use—the first local woman to pluck her eyebrows and wear lipstick. Faux pearls. In one hand-tinted photograph she wore a fur stole, bobbed hair, and a Garboesque hat. Her acid wit meant her dealings with men went strictly by her terms.

I once saw a tree fall. The feeling was like that. Within the past year, she had taken to the worrisome habit of leaving her house and crawling about outside, never mind the time or weather. It wasn't that she was deliberately neglected, however. The trouble was that she had to be watched constantly. The minute you turned your back, she was out the door. The responsibility could wear anyone down.

"I'm sick of the hour commute to Gallup, and then this happens," Grace said, sitting down across from me at the table. "I suppose I'll have to call in."

"No, don't do that," Frank told her. "I'll saddle up first thing in the morning. I'll find her."

Frank stood in the kitchen doorway holding their youngest daughter, Faith, who was fast asleep. He carried her into the other room and Grace sighed looking after them. She glanced at me, and I knew what she was thinking. Frank had been unemployed for over three years now, ever since the uranium mines had closed. He'd gone around town with references from the employment office, but finally he had stopped knocking on doors. He never said anything about it, but I knew. It was easier to stay away from town than face the humiliation. You didn't have to see the wealth and they way they treated people.

We walked a razor's edge. What else could we do? Every day we faced the theft, the lies, and the hate. And there weren't too many things to do about it. Either you smiled and pretended it didn't matter, withdrew to where they couldn't reach you, or kissed ass. Or you went under. Half the boys I'd known in grade school were dead. The list was long: Despair. Self-hate. Alcohol. No work and plenty of time to stew. How would any man feel? He didn't have to tell me why he didn't meet the gaze of the rednecks in town, the tourists who asked to take his picture, or the contemptuous social workers who didn't understand.

"It's totally crazy," Grace said. Frank came back and sat next to her. "They're asleep," he said, indicating the children in the next room with a nod of his head.

"It's a dirty shame," said Frank. "In the old days, old folks stayed with family to the end."

"That's the old days," sighed Grace.

"Dead and buried," said Frank, shaking his head.

"Gone with the buffalo," I said.

Frank looked at me. He grinned. "Belly up," he said, holding out his hand, palm up, wiggling his fingers.

"A bum deal," I said.

"The shits."

"A crying shame."

"Honestly, you guys," Grace said.

"Just awful," said Frank, and eyed her sideways.

Grace made a funny sound and her shoulders began to jerk up and down. I thought she was crying, but she wasn't. "Utter tragedy," she gasped, and her throaty laugh swept us up. Soon we were whooping and snorting at the absurdity of us flopping helpless as hooked fish in the language.

After we calmed down, Grace brought more coffee and a plate of muffins. "Amazing, isn't it?" she said. "It started with Dick-and-Jane. Now it's ship-the-old-lady-off-to-the-home."

"The Golden Years," Frank said.

"Shady Pines," I said.

"Okay, you two, that's enough," said Grace. "Let's get serious."

"If your sisters weren't such hang-around-the-fort Indians, you would have some help," Frank said.

"Now, hon," Grace smiled. "They're making good money. You know they can't get that kind of lab work around here. And they'll help with the cost too, you know."

"I wish I could do something," Frank leaned back and ran his hand through his hair.

"You have the cattle to look after. I don't know what we'd do if we didn't have the calves to sell in the fall. Besides, you look after the little ones when there's no sitter. How can I expect you to do all that and watch her too?"

As I sat there listening to them, I smelled the sharp odor of drying roots and wool. I heard the roof creak with the force of the wind. It was midwinter and I was about five years old. *Shimá sání* stood by the woodstove stirring something in a pot. The room was steamy and warm. She spoke in a quiet voice, describing in our language how her grandmother had told of surviving the forced march to Fort Sumner, three hundred miles to the east. A hundred years after it had happened, the tragedy was fresh in her mind. "It was cold like that," she'd said, pointing with her lips toward the window to indicate the freezing wind outside. "The people walked the whole distance at gunpoint. Many bad things happened. If anyone paused to rest, they were shot. A woman who had stopped to give birth was impaled on a sword. Old people were abandoned and babies were clubbed. Vultures followed them all the way."

I drowsed on her lap, the crackle of the fire inside the iron stove lulling me within the womblike embrace of her arms. The kerosene lamp cast a soft light on the log walls of her house.

There was a loom by her bed and she spent long hours each day weaving precious inches onto the rugs she made to sell. I played around her, making roads for my toy cars on the dirt floor. I stayed with her while my mother was at the hospital, a mysterious place I knew nothing about. After a while, she carried me to the bed and covered me with a quilt. Then she blew out the lamp and I went to sleep.

I saw what I had to do. "It's really for the best," I lied. "I mean, it's not doing her any good being out there. Think about winter, the storms, the hot stove. And you won't be the first ones to do it."

The words scraped my throat. Can you believe it, I thought. But these were modern times. The stars had shifted, my grandfather once said, and he didn't know what that meant.

The sink made a gurgling noise. We turned and saw ourselves in the window above the counter. The small dark panes fractured our faces into a strange mosaic.

"Remember last month when she almost picked up that baby rattler?" Frank said. "At least she'll be safe in Chinle."

"Safe," sighed Grace. "Who would have thought that she would turn into a child and that I would be the parent?"

"We have to do it, Grace. There's no choice." Frank touched her hand. A surge of anger rose inside me. They would never stop. The changes. The meddling. We were all affected, the men, the women, the children, and now the elders.

I glanced up and saw Frank and Grace looking at me.

"Damn it," Grace said.

I studied the veins on the back of my hands.

The alarm rang at four. I rolled out of bed and quickly got dressed. I went out to greet the dawn with prayer and pollen. Then I put on the coffee and watched the all-night news on TV while I waited for sunrise. In New York City, African Americans were protesting the killing of one of their young men by bat-wielding skinheads. The body of an undercover drug agent had been discovered in a shallow grave in Mexico. Outside, the rooster crowed and the clouds to the east slowly turned orange and pink.

The dog gruffed once and the gate hinges squeaked.

Frank opened the door and came in. He rubbed his hands together and grinned.

"I found her," he said. "She was in that culvert under the bus road. Shit, I passed by there twice yesterday and didn't think to look inside it. She's home now, sipping coffee and munching warm tortillas like nothing happened." He laughed and shook his head. "That old lady is really something . . ." He looked out the window.

I couldn't help it. I smiled.

I poured two cups of coffee and we watched the rest of the newscast. A suspended walkway in the atrium of the Kansas City Hyatt Regency had collapsed, killing several people and trapping scores of others under tons of steel and concrete. In Brazil, the Yanamamo were protesting the destruction of their forest homeland. On the other side of the world, the Maori were threatening to disrupt a visit by the Queen.

Meat and the Man

The wind, which had been blowing for several days, sullying the postcard blue skies of northwest New Mexico with dust, whistling through a million crevices in a thousand canyons, scouring out countless rainwater basins, moaning like a spirit in agony on the wires of power lines stretched across the plains, pushed against a lone car headed south on highway triple-six, which runs from Shiprock to Gallup. Jill Begay had dropped off her son at a friend's place and was driving home.

It was Sunday, and after Garth finished singing his latest hit on the radio, Father Cormac came on with "The Padre's Hour."

"*Haa'isha' diyin bizaad hani'aahgo, aa'ánílééh,*" he intoned, while a fragment of music from the *Diné* Blessingway played softly in the background. "*Áa'aaníinii náá dei yídiíl tah.*" The

245

sacred, written truth. But she was scarcely aware of the padre's words this morning.

The Flagstaff thing was really bothering her. She was thinking about the strange murder case that had been on the news lately. A *Diné* woman brutally killed in Flagstaff, stalked and ambushed in the parking lot of the hospital where she worked. The *bilagáanaa* man apprehended in the case claimed that a Navajo witch had done it, and the papers were referring to it as the "Skinwalker Defense." Suspicious clues, painted chicken bones and sticks, had been found at the scene of the abduction. The woman had been strangled with a belt and numerous bite marks were discovered on her body, the police said. She had fought desperately for her life. Now an all-*bilagáanaa* jury had acquitted the accused.

"*Hádéé sha' yigáálgo, át'í?*" Jill wondered. "*Jooba' daatsi á'áyisí hwee ádaadin.*" The latter clues, the belt and bite marks, bothered her. A so-called Navajo witch wouldn't do that, she thought. They don't have to lay a hand on you. They work their magic from afar. Violence was not their modus operandi.

She was so preoccupied with these thoughts that she almost didn't see the frantically waving *bilagáanaa* standing in the middle of the road. *Yáadilá!* she cursed, as she swerved just in time to avoid hitting him. The last of that morning's coffee slopped out of the cup snuggled in its holder on the door and splattered on her leg. "Son of a bitch!" she yelled as she veered around him, but several hundred feet down the road she stopped and, muttering to herself, put the car in reverse. She zigzagged back toward the man, who was now running toward her, his arms pumping madly. She noticed that in the stiff headwind, he was moving more up-and-down than forward. His windbreaker and chinos flapped wildly, and his thin gray hair appeared to be struggling to escape downwind.

At last, he stopped beside her car and the electric windows whined down slowly. "Ya-ta-hey!" he gasped, one hand clutching his round belly.

"*Aoo*," she answered, surprised somewhat by his attempt at *Diné bizaad*. People could sneak up on you like that. There were all kinds around. She couldn't help but be reminded of Father Cormac's dulcet tones, his trademark accent undiminished through five decades of work among *Diné*. The padre was still learning, though, always practicing. This man outside struggling to catch his breath nearly had the padre's unique intonation.

As a secretary for the Navajo tribal police, Jill met and dealt with many *bilagáanas*; she knew that their knowledge of *Diné* culture and their command of *Diné bizaad* ran the gamut. None of them, however, could hope to fool her. And *she* couldn't pretend to approach the verbal magic of the elders. This guy huffing and puffing outside her window had been around *Diné* before, she guessed. He at least knew the proper greeting.

Jill smiled. The guys at work had devised a code, a way of classifying visitors. Jokes. The best ones were reserved for full-fledged masters of *Diné bizaad* who could appreciate all the nuances. Middling jokes were served up to salesmen and the like. John Wayne jokes were delivered to the utterly hopeless. She tapped her fingers absentmindedly on the steering wheel as the man stood wheezing outside her passenger side window.

"My car, flat tire," he gasped, and surprised her by pointing down the road with his lips in the local manner. "Spare, flat too."

Jill couldn't help but feel sorry for the guy. His grandfatherly countenance touched her. He could be her *chei*, except she already had one and this guy was *bilagáana*. "Get in," she said, leaning over and opening the passenger door. "Looks like you could use a hand."

"Thanks," he said. "I mean, ahee—" But that's all he managed to get out before he started coughing. He pulled a hankie from his back pocket and dabbed at the corner of his mouth. She saw his eyes flutter and water up a bit as a strong gust swirled up dust. He looked soft, harmless as a teddy bear.

247

"*Ahéhee*," she finished for him. "And you're welcome."

"Oh, yeah," he said. "My little buddy." He pulled a shivering furball from inside his jacket. "This is my sidekick, Meat." Meat was a near-naked brown chihuahua. His watery eyes bulged at her, and his little pink member was slowly unsheathed as he wagged his tail.

Jill looked quickly away. "Cute dog," she said.

"His name's Meat."

"How odd."

"His full name's Grabs-the-Meat. A Navajo buddy of mine named him that because Meat has this habit . . . Uh, never mind." Jill looked at the man, and it was his turn to look away in embarassment. What a way to start off, she thought. Meat grinned at her. Then she suddenly became acutely aware of the feel of the coffee evaporating from her bare leg. The man patted the little dog's head absently.

They arrived at his car moments later, and after a few minutes of struggle they managed to get the tire off and into the back of her Jeep Cherokee. Then they turned around and headed back toward Shiprock.

They dropped off the tire at Chee's Texaco and went to the nearby restaurant to wait, a fried chicken place and a burger joint under one roof. Inside, a wall of glass separated the two sides. Jill started toward the entrance to the fried chicken place, but she saw he was heading toward the other door. She was about to say something when he announced, "C'mon. Lunch's on me." Meat was tucked inside his jacket.

The menu above the counter was a nightmare. Frybread, french fries, onion rings, fish sticks, tater tots. She felt her blood turning viscous. Some Navajo, she chided herself. She glanced through the glass partition. "I think I'll have chicken today," she told him. "They have skinless pieces." He looked surprised, but he nodded and smiled. He wasn't ready to concede, however. "Look," he said, "Navajo tacos. Care for one?"

She shook her head politely.

"Sure?" he prodded.

"I had one yesterday," she lied.

She got her platter and joined him at a table. They ate in silence for a while, suddenly awkward with each other. The wind creaked the big plate windows. She saw that the other customers were casting discreet glances at them. He noticed this and winked knowingly. He seemed to take their interest as a cue of sorts and openly enjoyed his taco, making exaggerated appreciative noises. "Mmm-mm-mm," he said. "This frybread is too good for words."

She peeled the crust from her chicken breast and barely stifled an urge to giggle. He smiled and cocked an eyebrow.

"Health, wealth, and lean," she explained.

"I've always loved this part of this country," he said. "There's something so *magical* here—I can't even begin to describe it."

Jill ignored the bounding tumbleweeds and bits of trash flying past, the crusty old Pamper that careened into the glass behind his head and bounced away. Twelve miles to the southwest, the twin jagged peaks of Shiprock rose serenely above the michievous wind frolicking on the plains below, gleefully lifting women's skirts and throwing dirt into people's eyes.

"What do you do?" he said, startling her.

"What?"

"Do you work?"

"I'm a secretary."

"Oh."

"Your turn," she said. "What do you do?"

"Uh," he said, but just then Meat whined softly. "Show the pretty lady what you can do," he said, dangling a bit of frybread over the little dog's head. Meat rose up on his hind legs. "Dance," he commanded. Meat panted and turned in little circles, nails clicking on the tiles, his tiny paws held to his chest in a beggar's pose. "Roll over . . . Play dead," he said, but Meat snatched the morsel and disappeared under the table. Jill crossed her ankles and tucked her feet back.

"How long have you had him?" She speared a bit of vegetable with her plastic fork and pointed at the dog with it.

"About ten years. From puppyhood, anyway. I'm his papa. I've made him the dazzling performer that he is." Meat sneezed underneath the table.

"That's a nice car you have," she said, but stopped, puzzled and embarrassed, when he blinked and looked away.

"She's old, but she gets me around," he said. "I call her Dotsy. That means 'maybe' in Navajo."

"I think I've seen one just like it around," she said. "Then again, there aren't too many gold Volvos hereabouts."

"I like unusual names," he said.

"Like *Daats'í?*"

"I'm just touring, to answer your question. You could say I'm a man of independent means. I come through here every now and then to relax, soak up the scenery. I drive around until I get my fill, then I take it with me. Sustains me, you know?"

"I know what you mean. I went to school in Phoenix and the trips back home are what helped me get through. Those visits recharged my batteries."

They finished the rest of the meal in silence, occasionally giving a scrap to Meat, who finally came out from under the table.

Just before they left, the girl behind the counter finally noticed Meat. "Hey, mister," she said. "No dogs allowed!"

Back at the car, they managed to get the tire back on with the help of Jill's cousin, Tony, who just happened by. He was tall, and the *bilagáanaa* craned back his neck to look up at him.

250

Tony tilted back his straw cowboy hat and narrowed his eyes at her mischievously. Then he waggled one eyebrow for punctuation. Meat, who had climbed astride the Volvo's steering wheel, yipped furiously but soundlessly behind the tinted glass. The man pulled a couple of bills from his wallet and offered them to Tony, but Tony shook his head. *"Na'nízhoozhgó yisháál,"* he told her with a wink. He patted the dirt off his hands, got back into his truck, and roared away with a backhanded wave.

Then they were alone and the silence of the land crowded around them.

"Well, I guess I'll be going," she said. "Thanks for lunch."

The guy cleared his throat and stood looking down the road. "It's getting late," he said. There was more than an hour of sunlight left. Meat did something to toot the Volvo's horn and the man glanced at the car. Still, he didn't make a move to leave.

Uh-oh, she thought, this getting just a little bit weird. I hope he's not one of those peculiars. "Well," she said again. "I'll be off now. Have fun touring." She looked back once in the rearview mirror and saw him gesturing; perhaps to Meat, or maybe to the wide blue sky. *"Yáadilá,"* she sighed. And then the road pointed her in the right direction toward home.

The wind stopped just before sunset, and a deep calm settled over the land. The western sky went gold and red. Jill was relieved to get home and had forgotten the earlier encounter with the man on the highway when she saw two vehicles approaching. She was chopping vegetables for the mutton stew they were having for supper. At the table behind her, her mother and grandmother sat peeling potatoes and sipping coffee. They saw her freeze and then lean forward, squinting out the window. They glanced at each other.

"Ha'á'tíílá?" her mother asked.

"Ch'íindii!" Jill exclaimed, dropping the colander full of cut celery, onions, and carrots into the sink. Some of the orange

disks of raw carrot bounced out and wobbled in circles on the countertop. Her husband Jim's red dually was coming down the narrow dirt road leading to her house, and behind it, the gold Volvo with tinted windows.

Jim had a big grin on when he came walking in the door, but it faded when he saw her expression. Uh-oh, his face said. What did I do? his eyes said. Then he understood. "Uh, honey," he said, "guess who's coming to dinner?"

"*Yá'át'ééh*," she said.

"Honey, this is—" Jim said.

"We've met," Jill said, surprising him.

"Ya-tah-hey, again," the man said. "Meat's in the car," he added, when he saw that question on her face.

"Well, welcome to my humble home," she said. "Supper won't be ready for some time yet. Why don't you show him around, Sweetie?"

Jim was coming from a full day of work and was probably tired too, but he nodded. He knew it was his mistake. He was kind-hearted, which was why she married him, but that got him into trouble now and then. Like now. And he understood that. And she had said "Sweetie" in that tone of voice.

"*Yáadilá óolyé*," her mother and grandmother exlaimed as she told about her day. They clucked their tongues and giggled. They loved a good story. This one hadn't ended. Maybe Jim had done them a favor.

"I nearly ran him down. He was flapping his arms like this," Jill said, imitating the man. "I almost didn't see him in time."

Outside, Jim and the man were at the woodpile chopping wood for her mother and grandmother's house next door. The man stood with hands idle in his pockets, watching as Jim swung the ax and sent the wood chips flying. They were talking about something. Jim stopped now and then to talk briefly and then he would heft the ax again. He pointed here and there, explaining things, establishing directions, outlining stories.

"I thought he was going to ask about our mating habits," Jim said later, when the man was in the bathroom washing up for supper.

"*Ma'ii*," exclaimed her grandmother, who wasn't supposed to hear that. She was setting the table. She wore slippers and walked quiet as a cat. She could scare the fur off a bear, Jim had complained more than once. Her mother was outside gathering the children, herding them toward the house.

"He *is* rather odd," Jill agreed.

The stew was delicious and everyone had seconds. The children were boisterous and full of questions. "What's your name?" they chimed. "What's your doggie's name? He looks like a mouse, a big mouse with no hair! Ew, look at his thingie! Mommy, I can't eat now. Look at his thingie! Gross!"

"Hush," Jill scolded. "Be nice. This is our guest."

"Our guess!" they chanted. "Our guess!"

Their guest was not offended and chatted amicably with everyone. After they were done, he insisted on helping with the dishes and Jill left him with the older women. He stood at the sink drying, while her mother washed and Grandma wiped the table and put away the dishes. Jill lay on the bed in her room for a few minutes, telling her muscles to relax. She listened to the soothing splash of water as Jim showered. When he came out, she decided to ask him how he'd come across the man.

"He flagged me down. Seems ol' Chee did a lousy job repairing his tire. Says he hadn't gone more than a mile when it went flat again."

"Did he point with his lips?"

"What?"

"Point with his lips—like this."

The industrious workers in the kitchen heard the sound of laughter coming from the back bedroom and glanced at each other. After a moment of silence, they resumed talking.

"So, after mission school at Saint Catherine's in Santa Fe, I came back home and got married," finished Grandma.

"And had me," added Jill's mother.

"And eight others," said Grandma.

"And she's got dozens of grandkids now."

"I have my own tribe right here," said Grandma.

"What about you?" said Jill's mother, turning to the man. "Are you married?" Just then, Meat created a diversion with his odd little dance. They ladies ohhhed and ahhhed. "Isn't he darling?" they said to Jill and Jim, who came back into the room to see what was going on. Together they drifted into the living room for their usual evening of television. The children were already sprawled on the floor, belly down, feet wagging in the air. Jim began his usual remote-controlled hunt through the channels when Grandma interrupted.

"This is rude," she said. "We have a guest. It's inconsiderate to ignore our guest and just watch television. Turn that thing off. Let's tell stories instead. He's interested in hearing some old-time stories. That's what he said."

"That's right," added Jill's mother. "They watch too much television anyway. When I was a child, there was no television. We told stories in the evening instead. That's our culture. We tell stories."

"Awww . . ." said the children as the screen went black. "We don't want no stories. Mom! Dad!"

"Your grandmother is right," Jim said. He shot a conspiratorial look at Jill. "Stories can be much better than television."

"Yeah, right," the children said.

"Especially skinwalker stories," Jim said, and the kids squealed. The women looked at each other. The man put down his coffee cup and leaned forward slightly. The children bunched together and sat looking up at their father with big round eyes.

"I hope they don't have bad dreams," Jill said as they were getting ready for bed. "Those scary stories used to give me nightmares."

"It's not them I'm worried about," Jim said, indicating with a nod of his head the nearby *hooghan* where the man had retired earlier. "I hope *he* can handle it."

"You know what would be funny? What if that stupid mule were to come around again tonight?"

"The trash thief?"

"Uh-huh." Then they were laughing again. The mule, a raggy old thing, had been coming around at night lately, raiding their trash barrel and causing a ruckus among the dogs. Jim had nearly shot the animal one night, until he shone his flashlight on it and saw what it was.

Inside the *hooghan*, the man was busy. He was scribbling furiously on a yellow legal pad. He muttered to himself as he wrote. He paused now and then to consider a word or a phrase. Meat was sullen and lay curled up on the bed nearby. He knew when he was playing second fiddle. The man worked for a while, then he finally lay down his pad and pen and sighed. He smiled and nodded at Meat. "It's been a good day," he said.

A little past midnight, the man woke. His bladder was nearly bursting. He lay motionless for a while, deciding, then he swung his legs over the side of the bed. He made his way to the door in the darkness, feeling his way with his bare feet. Outside, he sighed his relief and gazed up at the stars. Will you look at that? he thought, his mouth dropping open at the sight. The stars were incredible. The Pleiades. Orion. The Big Dipper. He was standing there awestruck, gaping at the beauty, when the dogs started barking suddenly and charged into the night. They were definitely after something. The man quickly finished and headed back toward the door, but in the darkness he couldn't see where the door was on the round *hooghan*. He didn't know that he passed by it until he knew for certain he'd gone too far. He turned and had started back the other way, when he heard the dogs coming back. They were running fast toward him. The man froze. The dogs were frantic. He strained to see and hear. The dogs suddenly were on the other side of the *hooghan*, then he heard heavy footsteps and loud, rapid breathing. Then something big and black loomed up in front of him, pursued by the frenzied dogs. He saw a pair of upright ears and smelled something foul. "Dear heaven, no!" The man put out his hands, wobbled, and fainted. Meat yipped savagely inside the *hooghan*. The mule jumped over the fallen man and disappeared, kicking and braying, back into the night.

Jim clicked on the porch light and yelled at the dogs to shut up. Then he noticed the man lying on the ground, his pale bare skin and skivvies glowing in the darkness. He shouted to Jill to get a flashlight and dashed out. He arrived beside the man just as the guy was coming to. The man saw Jim bending over him and screamed. "Easy there," Jim said. "It's me, Jim. That was a mule you saw. A mule that's been coming around to raid our trash barrel."

"What happened?" Jill said, hurrying up. "Did you trip, did you fall?"

The man quietly got to his feet. "Yeah," he said, "I tripped. I fell. I'm sorry if I woke you. I didn't mean to yell." Meat came bounding out and stood quivering with rage at their feet. He looked at each of them and they looked down at the little dog.

"Shut up, you idiot," muttered the man.

"I told you not to tell those stories," Jill said, as they watched the man drive away the next morning. "I think you just about scared that man to death. What if he'd had a heart attack?"

"He was awfully nosy," said Grandma.

"But he talked Navajo," Jill's mother said.

"Barely," corrected Grandma.

"I'll bet he never forgets last night," said Jill.

"Yup," said Jim. "He nearly shit his pants. You should have seen him."

"*Yáadilá*," said Jill.

"I thought he was nice—and rather good-looking, if you ask me," said Grandma. "What did you say his name was again?"